# YOU NEVER KNOW

# YOU NEVER KNOW

by Preston K. Franklin

Cover Art by Shondra C. Longino

ISBN: 978-0-692-75655-3

First Printing July 2016
PKF Publications
Printed in the United States

10  9  8  7  6  5  4  3  2  1

# Acknowledgements

First I would like to thank God and my Lord and Savior, Jesus Christ.

Thank you, Rosemary Rozell, for keeping me grounded through life. When I was up or down, you were there. Renea Davis and Dimitra McKissic, thank you for holding me down for five.

Latasha Cook, thank you for inspiring me to write the book. Her words were, "If you're through with the music, then use your creative mind to write a movie or a book." Well Latasha, I did.

I would like to also thank Gail Ife Young and my entire family from the Franklins to the Rozells to the Kellys in Chicago. I want give a shout out to the CPC clique, and Pitbull Territory for letting me express my creative mind. They taught me to never give up on trying to be successful. Shout outs to Jason Clark, Tamir and everyone else that stood by my side through tough times in Marion.

Shout outs to my homies Brano and Downtown Kenny Brown, Channing Lane and everyone else at the field that I rocked with. To my homies Bravo and Wayne, hold your heads up. Big Chris, hold your head up.

Special thanks to Shondra Longino for helping to put the finishing touches on this project.

To my girl, Buddah and the Prude family. To Lo, Bo, Trix, TJ, Jay Smooth, P, C, Dill, Bill, Psych, Trennace, Onie, Rozell, C.J., D.T., and Peace.

Peace and love.

Signing off.

You never know . . .

# DEDICATED TO:

*Those who are prisoners of the game,*
*known and unknown.*

*Those who are and have been incarcerated because*
*of the game.*

*Those who have suffered ills and misfortunes due to playing the*
*game.*

*Those who have lost lives and loved ones as a result of the*
*game.*

*Those who have chosen to walk away from the game.*

# Chapter 1

"Ta, that shit is sweet. Go on in there and get out. I'ma be waiting right over there for you," Peaches said.

"That shit's sweet, huh?" I replied.

"Yeeah, sweet!" she said; her eyes wider from being excited.

"Sweet, right?" I said again, more sarcastically this time. I sat in the back seat with a Chrome .45 resting on my lap.

See, I'm from Cleveland. And out of the twenty-seven years that I've been living here, I came to realize that ain't shit sweet. But what she didn't know was that it don't even matter, 'cause I got a newborn baby on the way and I'm on my way to the homeless shelter.

But my predicament is about to change. My cousin out here killing 'em in these streets and he ain't trying to cut a nigga in. And on top of that, I've been rocking these Nike boots for at least a year. Yeah, and them boys are leaning.

So whether this shit is sweet or not, I'm going in. I'm doing this. And once I get past that door it ain't no turning back…

ONE YEAR LATER…

*Call from Felicia,* my phone's computerized voice announced.

"Yeah, what up?" I spoke into my phone.

"What's up? You tell me what's up," Felicia said.

"Shiit, I'm going to the Phase tonight and you already know that a nigga gone be Mauri shoe gator and Lacoste out."

"Mauri and Lacoste? Hah! Nigga, stop playing, 'cause they already told me that Rino made you__

"Tuck my chain?" I said, cutting her off. "Yeah, I heard that too-but look; you tell Rino, or whoever the fuck said that bullshit, that they got me fucked up." Sitting in my car, parked, I ran my hand over the steering wheel trying to stay calm. "These V.V.Ss in my shit have been known to bring the rain out," I added.

"So what you saying is that your diamonds is like lightning?" Felicia asked. I could hear her smacking her lips.

"Hell yeah! And you already know that shit, right?" I leaned back in my seat. "Man, what's up, doe? Is you gone meet me up there or not?"

"Ta, why do you call everybody a *man*?"

"It's just something like a noun or something. It stands for people, places, and things," I said and chuckled.

"Do I look anything like a man to you?" she asked.

She was right, doe. Felicia was one of the finest bitches I knew. Light brown skin, hazel eyes, real hair, long legs, long lashes, and some full lips with a fat ass. But I know when a chick is feeling me and for some reason I just wasn't getting that type of feedback from her. At least not the kind that I wanted.

"Look," I said. "I'ma keep it real, Felicia. If I'm pushing and you're pulling, then we're only gonna end up falling. So you got my number. If you trying to slide then call me and don't wait until I'm up there. Shit, they only have this set once a year." I paused but not long enough for her to answer. "Alright holla," I said and hung up the phone. As soon as I hung up it rang right back. "Hello." I picked up before the caller could be announced.

"Ta, what's up? This Slick."

"Shiit, silking it, my nigga. So Slick what's up with you?"

"Man, not too much. I know you going to the party, Ta. What's up?"

Yeah, this was my nigga, Slick. The type of nigga that you'll have to worry about. You. Not me. 'Cause see, this was my nigga for life. And I knew his M.O., pretty but gritty. "Yeah Slick, you know I'ma breeze through there."

"Breeze through there? Ta, what the fuck you think? What? You some type of celeb or something?"

I chuckled. "I been a celebrity for years. Now I'm on President status, ya hear me?"

"Man, quit capping, Bleed. And what time is you talking 'bout shooting up in that bitch?"

"In a couple, Slick. Matter fact, I got a few moves to make so just meet me up there."

"Oh yeah, Ta. I almost forgot to ask you. What's this shit I hear about soft ass Rino making you tuck yo chain?"

"Man, stop! You know me, my nig, so let's end the speculation right now." Then I figured I should explain. "I'm at the gas station right when the friendly roll up in that bitch." Slick was letting me know he was listening to the story, saying, 'right, right.'

"I didn't want to look all hot, 'cause when I pulled up I already had the windows down with the system bumping and big Kush packs all in the trunk." I started up my car while I was talking. I put the phone on speaker and pulled off.

"Friendly was in the lot looking for somebody like four cars deep with their sirens on," I said, turning the corner onto 131st Street. "So I got out the car and threw the Dolce frames on the seat and put my chain in my shirt. Then this nigga blow down on me with some ole big goofy ass shit around his neck. And the nigga's medallion was too thin to win, you hear me? Fugayze. No lumps. No chunks." Slick laughed.

"And to make it so bad," I continued, "this nigga still walked to me and had the nerve to try to buy some smoke. The nigga's straight up lame. I'll kill that nigga if I…"

"Whoa!" Slick interrupted.

Good thing he did 'cause I mighta said something I shouldn't on the phone.

"Yo Ta, I'ma see you up there, bet?"

"Bet."

I hung up the phone, riding, thinking. I turned onto Kinsman. *"Tuck my chain."* That nigga probably tucked that wire he was wearing.

The shit was starting to piss me off and I don't even know why because him and his brother was some straight lames.

"Man, if I see that nigga…" I said out loud. I bit my lip and shook my head. "Naw, I hope I *don't* see that nigga 'cause I'll fuck around and bust on him."

I smiled. Yeah, 'cause the only person that I'm trying to bust on tonight is Felicia.

I glanced over at the passenger seat. Two ounces of water, a bottle of Belvi and some Kush. "Yeah, it's going down." My grin spread across my face. "A young playa is about to be wasted."

I still had a few drops to make 'cause the set didn't start for another four hours. Niggas had already been calling me for these pounds. And me and my little nigga had to go and get that bread. Yeah, my little nigga, 4nick. He stayed with me around the clock. All day. Every day.

"So how much?" asked Luth.

"Luth, you deal with me every week. Sometimes, twice a week. So why do you keep asking me how much like the shit changed?" I had pulled up in front of a house near 125th and Kinsman and was sitting in my car with the window rolled down.

"You heard, Ta. Like you said, I deal with you twice a week sometimes, so therefore, the prices should go down for me," Luther shot back. He stood outside my window.

"Luth, how can I drop prices when the price of gas keeps going up?" I looked up at him. "Okay, this is what I'll do. I'ma bring you back something else. It's kinda the same but just a little less potent, 'cause shit, I'm getting super taxed for this shit."

"Naw, man," Luth said, shaking his head.

"What you mean, 'naw?'"

"I mean-my people was loving the first shit. So here. Give me two," he said, handing me a roll of money with rubber bands around it.

"Yeah. I know they was loving that shit so why is you breaking my balls complaining?"

"Take this money, you dirt bag." Luth shoved the money through the window but had a smile on his face.

"Ahhh! I'ma dirt bag, huh? Well, I've been called worse."

"Oh yeah, Ta," Luth said, changing the subject. "You going to the set?"

"What kinda question is that? Romell is hosting that bitch, too? Last year the young nigga had so many hoes in that bitch that the firetrucks was parked outside."

"For what? It was a fire hazard up in there or something?" Luth asked.

"Naw. Hell naw. Them niggas was trying to get in that bitch too." We both laughed. He leaned in and gave me some dap.

"I'ma holla at you at the set," I said.

"Love," we both said as I closed the window and rolled out.

# Chapter 2

Yeah, that was my nigga, Fat Luth. He thinks that he's my best custy but little does he know that this young nigga from down the way is buying like four of what he bought a week. But one thing about Luther, is the nigga is solid; a negotiating ass nigga, but he's solid. These other niggas I don't know from a can of paint. I ain't really trying to know them either because as much as I would like it to be, this game ain't nice. Believe me. My guards stay up. I stay strapped, and I'd rather get caught with it than without…

*You have an incoming call from…* I didn't let the phone finish.

"Hello," I said.

"Yeah, is you coming to get me or what?" Felicia's voice was soft.

"Oh, what you mean? You trying to slide now?"

"Yeah, boy, quit playing. Is you coming, Ta?"

"Shiit, the set don't start for a couple of more hours so why is you rushing me, girl?"

"'Caause…" she drew the words out. "Ladies get free drinks when they get in before ten," she explained, talking slow like she was retarded. Or maybe she thought I was the one that was retarded.

"Well, you won't be drinking for free then," I said, talking slow like she was.

"Ta?" Her whining was getting to me.

"What? Don't worry, Ma. Finish getting yourself ready and I'll be there about 11p.m. The set ain't over until 4a.m. anyway, so 'bout time we leave, I promise you that you gone be roasted."

"Yeah?" Felicia said, sounding happy.

"No bullshit," I assured her.

"Oh yeah? Do you remember Saree?"

I grunted. I remembered her vaguely.

"Well, she said she wants you to come pick her up too. And she said that she's trying to link up with one of yo' boys, so bring one wit'cha."

"Shiit. Tell her that it's gone be niggas at the spot. Fuck I look like? VibeLine?"

Felicia laughed and said my name in a sweet type of seductive voice. "Ta, do it for me."

"Damn. Look man, she can ride, but tell shorty don't be on that bullshit. Girly got a fly ass mouth and you know my niggas catch bodies and DVs," I said.

"Stop playing so much, Ta."

My phone beeped and I had to interrupt her. "Let me take this call on the other line. I'll see you in a minute." But before I ended the call with her, I added, "Tell yo girl to be ready too. And tell her that she better have something on the tank." I heard her get ready to start that whiny voice again. "Naw, I'm just fucking with you," I said, before she could say anything. "Just be ready, doe. Holla."

Felicia's girl, Saree, was tall with a perfect slender body. She had some pretty ass Chinese eyes but don't let those good looks fool you, 'cause see, she's been known to be on the passenger's side more than once while the driver was thinking that he was about to smash something and ended up getting his wig popped off.

Word on the streets is that she was setting niggas up and I wasn't ever the nigga to get robbed. But I definitely wouldn't put it past this broad because it used to be real coincidental that after she's on the passenger side screaming and crying, the next week she's sitting on new furniture, bigger spot, and a new whip.

Shit, doe, I ain't the police, so I hadn't been trying to solve no cases. I really didn't care what she did. But really, that bitch is a dime and she ain't got no nigga. What's wrong with that picture?

Still, I had to look out for my niggas. Which one of my nigga's is gone fuck with that hoe? I got four hours to put this shit together. I pulled over into BP on 116th and Shaker Blvd. and parked.

"Hello, Mike." I called the first of my niggas that came to mind. "What up, boy? Are you trying to slide with me, Felicia and her girl, to the set tonight?"

"Yeah, boy," Mike said. "I'm with that, Ta. But hold up. Who is her girl?"

"Saree."

"Saree? Man, hell naw! What you trying to get me? A case?" That didn't work out too well.

I searched through my contact list and found someone who I thought might be willing to double date.

"J.T., is you coming to the set?" I asked, when he answered the phone.

"Hell yeah. You already know what's up."

"You wanna roll with me, Felicia, and Saree, then?"

"Man, what's up, Ta? You trying to set me up or something?"

"Naw, nigga, you know it ain't like that."

"Well, I don't rob niggas either, so I can't believe that you even asked me that shit. That's the type of shit you into now?" J.T. sounded pissed as he ended the call.

Cross his name off the list. Shiit. Going through the contacts, I tried everybody that I could think of. Call after call after call...

"Hello."

"No!"

"Hello."

"No!"

"P. What's up, my nigga?"

"Fuck no! You must be smoking too much water, boy. You done finally lost yo rabbit ass min.' The only way that I would mess with that chick is if she was tied up and phoneless. Matter fact, let me call you back." Then he hung up on me too.

That shit was hopeless. My niggas stay getting money, and one of the reasons was that they don't fuck with hoes like her.

"Hello?" Felicia said, when I rang her up after calling everybody I could think of.

"Yeah, Felicia. What's up? I don't think your friend is gone be able to come," I said, before she could say anything.

"Damn. That's messed up, Ta. She's depressed 'cause her little brother just got killed last week on 84th Street," Felicia sighed in disappointment.

"84th? Oh yeah. I heard about that. A little nigga was sliding in an old school Monty, sitting up high, and the jack boys... Hold up for a second." I heard my other line beeping.

"Hello," I said, clicking over. "Who the fuck is this?"

"This Black, hoe ass nigga."

"Hoe ass nigga, what? I'll beat yo ass, bohhy. Remember you still my little nigga, and don't forget that."

I hadn't thought to call Black. "What the fuck you want, doe? I asked him.

"Yeah, Mike told me that you was out here playing matchmaker and shit, trying to get a niggas wig split fucking with that chick, Saree."

"Man, tell Mike's ole scary ass to take his ass to church, bohhy. What's up, doe? Do you need me to come see you?"

"Naw, Bleed. I still got some of that left, but you can come swoop yo nigga, 'cause you know I like girly."

"You like her, huh? You like her for real?" I smiled. "You dirt bag."

"Dirt bag? You the one trying to hook everybody up with the scandalous broad," Black said.

"I mess with Felicia, and I'm trying to do her a favor. And I'll be glad to let Saree know that you like her."

Yeah, Black probably did feel this chick, 'cause when I think about all the females that he had, they were all pretty much similar.

But I don't think none of them played the field like Saree. And believe me when I say, it was *real* in the field.

"Man, Black, is you sure that you can handle this hoe?"

Black's voice changed. He sounded real serious. "My nigga, I got this. I came off the porch early."

"Alright, man." I shook my head and chuckled to myself. "Just make sure that you keep this hoe off of my radar whenever I come swoop. Bet!"

"Bet. I got you. Just make sure that you got some good water for us to blow, 'cause you know I got half on whatever."

"Damn, bohhy. On whatever? That Eastside must be cranking. Alright I got that for you." Before we ended the call I said, "Love."

I clicked back over to Felicia. "Hello."

"Yeah, boy, you was 'bout to get hung up on," Felicia said, sounding irritated from keeping her on hold so long.

"Well, what's wrong with you hanging then?"

"Huh?" She seemed somewhat taken off guard by my smart comeback." She didn't say nothing for a minute. "Anyways," she said, "my girl is gonna be sad that she can't come, but__"

"Oh yeah…, she can come. My bad," I said, cutting her off. "My nigga Black, said that he been digging her for a minute."

"Who?"

"My nigga, Black," I repeated.

"Yo nigga, Black? What?" Felicia started laughing. "Black? That nigga is scant."

"Shit, not my nigga."

She was right, doe. My nigga was lightweight scant, doe. But he ain't never fucked me over before. And ever since we been swerving for the last six years, he ain't never asked me to front him nothing. Matter-of-fact, the young nigga put me back together when them people had stormed in my shit, and when that fat nigga K.B. dropped a dime on me. Yeah, guess who handled that shit, too?

"I don't know if she's gonna want to go with him, Ta," Felicia said.

"Look, she ain't got that many options, so__"

"Well, okay," Felicia said. "She should be cool."

"Felicia, I'm doing you a favor. This ain't really how I gets down. I basically just wanted to slide wit' you." I knew the bit of frustrations I was feeling showed in my voice.

"Okay. Thanks Bay. I'ma make it up to you. I promise that I'll make tonight worth it," she said, her voice softening. "I'll call you in a minute, so be ready, Ta." I hung up.

What's the infatuation that I have with this chick, I don't know. I mean, a nigga is polished, right? But I still don't mind riding with trouble. See, for some reason it just don't scare me. It ain't the fact that I stay strapped up, but it's just the drama. I've always been through it. I lived through it, and I know that in the game I'm in, it will always come back.

I started the car and headed back out to the streets to take care of my business.

# Chapter 3

I don't know..., I got a baby momma, a chick on the side, and I know that it's gone be beaucoup hoes at the set. Still, I wanted to bring a date.

See, I'm from Buckeye, and one thing for sure, two things for certain, is that we get money and know how to throw a fly set. And here I was, trying to be on a double date.

Three hours to the set, so I figured that I'll go pick up Black, first. I had to make a few more drops to this one lil' nigga down the way. The nigga was moving all that tree but still hadn't bought him no whip yet. Fuck it. I'll just blow down on him. My nigga, Blacks,' from down that way too. See, I tries to play shit smart.

"What up?" I had pulled up in front of Black's house and called him.

"Yeah, what up with that shit you was talking on the phone, nigga?" he barked into the phone.

"I'm outside, Bleed, so don't get scared and cop deuces now," I said, joking around with him. "Naw, but for real bohhy; what you got going?"

"I'm silking it until you pick me up for the set," he said.

"Man, didn't I say I was here? Come on outside."

"Ta, man, I told you that I still got some trees left. It's been kinda slow around here. Some niggas just got merked a couple of days ago."

"Man, I need you to take this ride with me real quick."

"Man, hold up. Let me lock up," he said. I hung up the phone.

Black came out the house, jumped in the whip, and gave me some dap like he was hyped up 'bout seeing a nigga.

"Hey, Man," he said and smiled. "Put something in the air."

"Man, I knew you was about to say that." I laughed and pulled off. "You got some squares?" I asked. I pulled a bottle out of my pocket.

"Naw," Black said. "Stop right here." He pointed to Ra-Ra's, the Arab corner store on the next block from him. "We can get some there." I parked and we got out.

I walked over to the cooler and grabbed one Arizona for me, and one for Black. Black walked past a few females and looked them over smiling. He walked up to the counter "Yeah, let me get a pack of Newport's, some Jolly Ranchers, the Ginsing... He grabbed the drinks out my hands and put them on the counter. "These Arizona's. Oh, and a box of rubbers."

Ra-Ra looked at Black, smirking. "Ooh, you about to get yo little jimmy wet, huh?"

Black came back saying, "Yeah, unlike you; 'cause you only get that big ass beard wet." Ra-Ra's mouth dropped opened. "Yeah, them broads already told me about you, Ra," Black added.

We went back to the car and Black didn't say anything for a minute. "Hey man," Black looked back at the store out of the corner of his eye then over at me. "Ra just tried to lightweight clown me."

"What?" I grabbed the bag from his hand.

"Naw, man, he was just joking around."

I handed him a bottle. "Here. Tap something."

"Hold up. Give me ten dollars first, Mister."

"I got half on whatever," I said.

"Daaamn, Thirst Mgurst! I was talking 'bout later," Black said.

"Nigga, now *is* later," I said. "Yeah, nigga, some of that."

"Well, we're starting early. Go ahead and take that bitch to the wilt," Black told me.

The wilt is the filter, and if you didn't know, we ain't smoking weed, we blowing water. And when I think about why I fucks with

Black so tough, then that's probably the main reason. Our D.O.C.s were the same.

My other niggas didn't smoke no water. But me and this nigga could grind high and didn't really care about what people thought about it. 'Cause see, when it comes down to it, I'ma crooked nigga, too. I just always done a good job in disguising it, you know? Polo downed, fresh haircut daily and clean whips and shit like that. At times I had to wonder if I was the shisty one. And sometimes I wondered too much, so I'd blow a stick and slow my thoughts down. I would just be quiet and grind and progress. You feel me?

Headed down Woodland toward the projects, I looked over at Black and said, "Man, you stuck, dude."

"No I'm not, Bleed. I'm cool," he said, sounding slightly defensive.

"Man, what good is you gonna be with me down here if you too high and can't react to nothing?"

"Bleed, I'm cool. I just told you." He looked at me with droopy eyes. "But why don't this little nigga meet you half way?" he said. "You been fucking with this nigga for over a year. He should have a whip by now." Black started rubbing his eyes, trying to wake up out of the mini zone. Then he added, "Man, it's something fishy 'bout this nigga if you ask me."

"Who you telling? You got yours, doe, right?" which was a dumb question, I knew. Because if this nigga didn't have a dime in his pocket, he'd still have that hammer on him. And he flosses that bitch like a city cowboy.

"Man, I ain't just got it__, this baby is cocked and ready to go," he replied.

Little Man seen me pull up. I switched up rides on him, but he still pent me in the gray Alero.

He pointed towards the back of the lot and that's where I went. He knew his projects better than me. When I pulled up, I backed in, looking at him and his niggas; shirts off, tatted up, and all of them niggas had gold grills in their mouths, too. I hoped they were grills and not perms 'cause this is still the Land, you know.

Lil'man came to the passenger's side. "What up, Ta? I see y'all smelling good in there." He was talking about the water scent that was still lingering in the car.

"Lil'man," I nodded my head at him. "What's up? What was you trying to do?"

"I need five of them, Ta," he said.

"You know the ticket, right," I asked.

"Shiit, if you ain't go up on me. I got twenty-five racks right now," he said. He was smiling chinky-eyed, patting his pockets like he was getting major paper.

I looked around the lot because this lil nigga be playing with some paper. His niggas was about five deep, but they wasn't tripping because if they was, they coulda got us when I first pulled up in the lot.

"Hey, grab that bag partner," I said to Black, which drew Lil'man's attention to Black.

"What's up, Black?" Lil'man said, grinning like the two of them had some type of rapport.

Black nodded his head at him, saying, "what's up?" Then he said, "I don't trust you nigga. I didn't fuck with you when I lived down here and I really don't fuck with you now."

I didn't comment on what Black said. I just kept it moving.

"Lil'man, here you go. Five of them," I said. "You want me to put them on the ruler for you?"

I knew that he'd say 'no' 'cause basically I haven't came up short, yet.

"Here go twenty five thousand," Lil'man said. "All hundreds," he boasted.

I gave it to Black. "Here. Count this out for me, Blizzy."

After about three minutes, Black looked over at me and said that it was all there. I pulled out the lot and my nigga was looking at me like he wanted to say something.

"What's wrong, Bleed?" I asked, turning down the player.

"Shiit, you lightweight using me, Cuz. All them niggas out there. Man, they coulda robbed the shit out of us. And what the fuck? I'm yo flunky now? Count this out for me, Blizzy." He mocked my words but I could tell he was serious.

"I knew it, Man. Quit crying with yo soft ass. That nigga paid full price for every pound. And I think the nigga's lightweight fishy myself and that's why I taxed him full price. So if something goes sour at least I was shooting for the skrilla. And you think I'ma have you come down here for no reason? Dude, on some real shit, I could've charged him four stacks for each pound just for him buying five pounds at once and that's twenty. But I charged him twenty-five. That made $5,000 extra profit. I'ma keep three," I said. "Here." I passed two stacks over to him. "You get two grand, hoe ass nigga, just for counting up some punk-ass paper. Ole spoil ass nigga. Now who else you know that makes two Gs in thirty minutes?"

Black looked at me smiling and said, "you nigga."

"Whatever, nigga. Let me get my ten on the square now. What's up with that? Oh yeah. I'm 'bout to drop you off and make a few moves." I looked over at him. "Get dressed and I come back and get you. And look. We're trying to kill 'em tonight, nigga, so don't be wearing no starter jackets and shit," I said, laughing.

"Nigga, quit playing."

"Naw, for real dude. Girly said she don't really know about you."

"Yeah?" he said. "Well, I'm doing that hoe a favor, so tell her any funny shit jump off, and I'ma pop her top, ya dig?"

"Man, you ain't gone pop nothing," I said, pulling up to his house. "I can tell that you in love with that broad already."

"Oh yeah? Ta, just don't wear that corny ass wind-breaker that you be grinding in to the set."

'Ahh! If I did, I'll still knock off more hoes than you."

# Chapter 4

I tapped a square half way with like two and a half hours until the set started. But for real, the way my celly kept jumping, it was starting to make me think like, 'fuck the set.' But the truth of the matter was that Romell only threw this set once a year. Plus I'm trying to link up with this diva that got me in a trance. I'm breaking my own rules for this chick, 'cause see, looks are deceiving. But it's something else about Felicia that makes me want to fuck with her all like that.

She'll hit a stick too. But she got dough for no reason. A daddy's girl and for real, it's been times that she looked out for me when I was dirt ball broke. And I think that's why I'm so into her right there.

I drove down Buckeye. *I got one more drop to make; to my old school nigga, Will*, I thought to myself. So before I got there I decided to smoke my square, and this time I sprayed some cologne.

Will was cool but he was nervous acting. I could understand, doe, 'cause the nigga had a house in the burbs, three cars, and was about to retire from his job in a year. Plus, he never been robbed or been in jail before and I wasn't 'bout to be the reason for any of that to happen.

I pulled up in Will's driveway. I saw him come out his side door, so I got out the car. "Will, what's up? What was you trying to do?"

Will didn't switch up much. He stayed in his safety zone and that's probably the reason that he never got caught up in shit. "Ta, I'm just trying to do my usual," Will said.

"Alright then. Here you go, ole buddy," I said.

"I want you to see something real quick, Ta."

"Man, Will, I really was trying to get in and out."

Will walked in the backyard and I followed. He opened the garage and took the cover off of a '72 Cutty, all black with chrome everywhere on it.

"Damn, OG! Who blessed you with this bitch?"

"Never mind that, Ta," he said, with a lightweight serious look on his face. "I'm trying to see if I'm gonna keep it or not. I need a second opinion on it to make sure that I'm going to keep it." He gave me a nod. "Eh Ta, I want you to take it for a spin for me."

"Man, Will, I wish I could, but I told you that I gots to get going. I gotta get ready for the hood set at the Phase 13. I'm running late as we speak."

"Look," he said. "I'll tell you what. Since you're my little nigga, do you want to drive it to the set tonight?"

That surprised me. "Huh?"

"Yeah. As long as when you drop it off you'll come by yourself."

My whip wasn't no slouch. I'm talking 'bout I had some pretty nice vehicles myself. I wanted to say 'no' but the little nigga came up out of me.

"Alright Will. I'll fill up the tank."

"Whatever, Ta. I just want your honest opinion on how it rolls."

Man, this nigga must be crazy, I thought. I mean you shoulda seen this bitch; all black and chrome. But everything on the inside was digital. Three hundred fifty Rocket engine that was chromed out; soft black leather seats with a slight tint, plus it had 30-day tags on that bitch. So the first thing that came to my mind was how Felicia was going to react when she see me in this.

I pulled my car all the way in the back and parked. I got the keys from him, opened up the door and slid into the leather seat.

"Ta, don't be getting no nut stains on my seats."

"Alright,, bet," I said, running my hand around the steering wheel.

"Matter-of-fact, just bring it back in the morning, young'un. Oh, and don't be smoking no water in it either, you hear me?"

"Yeah alright, Will." But I was thinking that if he knew like I knew, he'd know that I'm smoking a stick in this miraculous mothafucka.

"All right, Will," is what I said out loud. "You know I'ma take good care of this puppy like it was my own. Good looking out, Will."

I hit the freeway and shot to my duck off close to my Pop's crib. Pops got one of those mailboxes that goes directly into the house. I knew that he was probably drunk on the couch, so I slid three hunnit' in there and shot around the corner to my spot.

It didn't bother me when Pops was drunk or high 'cause he always looked out for me whenever I was down. So whatever he did, fuck it, you know? Who am I to judge anyway? That was my nigga for life.

I stepped inside of my house and shit was going off rip. Keep it plain, right? Bracelet not too big, VVSs, white gold and diamonds-$12,000. Dolce frames, all black-$1,250. Lacoste shirt with the big dumb-ass alligator on it, exclusive shit-$165. Diamond baguettes hanging, matching the bracelet on the 'thin grown man side.' All black Mauri's that I paid $1100 for, black hard Levis'-sixty-five dollars, and I took them back to Fahrenheit on the cologne side. The price on that didn't even matter, doe. See, dressing was an art where I'm from. I ain't one a those clowns out there trying to be fly every day. Shiit, I'ma man, so I like to be rough sometimes but when it's time to going out, then this is what I does. I mean my whole clique knew how to get fly.

I left my bedroom, and went downstairs. I looked at myself in the large mirror that hung in the living room with admiration.

*Like oh, how one color can look so good.*

# Chapter 5

I grabbed the Rozay bottle out of the small fridge and headed across to the big one. I grabbed the champagne for the breezies and then got some red Solo cups out the cabinet. Yeah, a nigga like me don't really drink that. That Belvi, doe, gone be right on time.

Locking up the house, I hopped in Will's Cutty and pulled off. I grabbed my cell phone and punched in a number. "Hello Black. What up, bohhy? Shiit is you ready?"

"Yeah, you already know," he said. "Man, where is you at?"

"I'm on the freeway. I'll be there in 'bout ten minutes."

"Eh, man, grab me a shell. I came across my one cat... Man, just grab a shell and I'll tell you about it when you get here."

I pulled up in the gas station. Damn, this bitch stay jumping. Flock of breezies ova there eyeing a nigga. 'Nice car,' one of the chicks said. She was staring at me.

"Not as nice as you," I shot back. "Good looking, Ma," I said and stepped into the store.

Quick conversation for the honey's but in all seriousness this ain't my hood, doe, so I'm trying to get in and out.

"What up, Ta? I ain't seen you in a while. Since high school, in fact."

I looked at the dude. He might've known me but I couldn't remember dude's name or his face.

"You don't even remember me, do you?" the stranger asked.

"Man, you know I'm lightweight geekin'. Plus, I tries not to remember too many people now days; you feel me?" I said, getting irritated with this guy for holding me up.

"That's your whip right there?" He nodded his head in the direction of the car.

I followed where he nodded. Looking through the window, I could see the Cutty. "Naw, it's a friend of mines," I said.

The store clerk said, "Can I help the next person," and I stepped past a couple of cats and squeezed through the stranger and his boys.

"Yeah, let me get two cigarillos, two Red Bulls, 20 Jolly Ranchers, four waters and that's it, boss."

"Need a bag?"

"I'm good," I said. I put the cigarillos and candy in my pocket and scooped up the drinks in my arms. Walking out, I bumped into dude again.

"Yeah, I'm Marco. Me and you was in 12th grade together," he said. "Yeah, doe, won't you sell me some of that good tree that you be having?"

"I ain't got none, Bleed," I said, trying to walk faster to the car so I could get dude out my face.

Marco seemed to get offended. "Oh, we blood now?"

"You know what I mean, Fam. It ain't no gang shit," I said, trying to keep walking towards the Cutty, but the nigga kept following me talking crazy.

"A nigga get a few dollas and all of a sudden they think they big time, right?"

At first I'm thinking, 'just do this nigga with the hands,' right? But then I thought, 'I might get my outfit dirty.'

'Just fuck it,' I decided. This shit ain't promised. "My nigga," I said. "I'll appreciate if you'll quit eyeballing me like a bitch."

I opened the door of the car, dropped my stuff in and grabbed my hammer. I turned back around and *bam! bam! bam!* I hit dude in both legs, jumped in the whip and peeled out.

Yeah, I knew that nigga! And his name wasn't Marco. And I had only made it to the 11th grade. That was Rico, a known jack boy from the Eastside. And the best thing about it was that I had my phone on neck clip, so I got that shit on video cam. I'ma about to trip on this shit for about a month. Fuck! What was he thinking? I told niggas that I'ma crooked nigga too.

I pulled up to Black's apartment complex and them bitches was cold from the inside out. I never ain't really asked him how he kept his shit up because he always kept the weed that I sold him. He's the slowest in the grind but he always kept some dough.

He came out in all black, head to toe, with a towel in his hand he used to wipe off his face.

"Man, Ta."

"What's up?" I asked him when he got in the car.

"She in there tripping," he said. "She found a few rubbers in my pocket and now she's in there going crazy."

Crazy wasn't the word when it came to Tona. That chick was *Beseeerk!*

Tona was yelling and throwing Black's clothes off the top porch. "And fuck you too, Ta," she screamed.

I leaned over and looked through the passenger window up to where she was. I shrugged my shoulders like, *Damn, what the fuck did I do?* "Man, I see what you were talking about earlier," I said, sitting up straight. Then I noticed Black's swag and said, "Damn, bohhy. I see you got some pieces on." I had to give him props on his jewelry.

The nigga came out mega fly. Blue diamonds off the black Izod, and Sean John. Not the bullshit Sean John either. Then he killed 'em with the Paris style apple hat.

Black was supposed to be showing me the weed, but seemed to be thrown off by the wheels.

"What the fuck, my nigga. You just copped that bitch?"

I smiled at him and nodded my head. "Man, that bitch is so raw," Black said. "What, you sold the truck or something?"

"Naw Man," I said. "It's just a favor from a friend. But them breezies ain't gotta know, right?"

"Riiight," Black said. I knew he felt where I was coming from.

"This bitch is mean, my nigga." Black was eyeing the interior of the car. "Come on." Black tapped his hand on the dashboard. "Let's peel before baby momma get to throwing more shit off the balcony."

"Bet." I said. "And I wanted to see what you were talking about, too."

I started up the Cutty and peeled. Black pulled out a nice looking weed sample and showed me.

"Oh yeah, my Arab nigga shot me this and told me to try it out. He said that his pounds is going for fifteen hundred but that's only if we get enough of them."

I looked over and said, "let me see that." I felt the bag and sniffed it. I started looking at the weed like a scientist.

"Yeah, this shit looks like or better than the stuff that we got now. But I wonder how it smokes." I glanced over at Black.

"Oh yeah, that chick Saree smoke trees, we'll have her test it."

Black looked back over at me and said, "Hell naw! She'll fuck around and get high and stuck, then she won't be trying to do nothing tonight. Look Ta, I say that we just get 'em, bang them bitches for five grand apiece and if a nigga got a problem, then we'll get them back on the next batch."

I handed him back the bag of weed. "That shit is real attractive, my nigga. You're probably right. Matter-a-fact, now that I think about it, you're absolutely right, I might say, Mate."

We laughed. Then Black said, "Damn my nig, what type of accent was that?"

"I don't know, nigga; French, Australian, whatever. Oh yeah, I just ran into a little drama at the Marathon."

"For real? What the fuck happened, Bleed?"

"You remember that nigga, Rico?"

"Think so," he said.

"Well, I think__ No hold up let me rephrase that. I *know* that the nigga was trying to rob me. Telling me his name was Marco."

Black looked over with a serious looking face and asked, "So what did you do?"

"Well, you know how the Marathon be jumping right? I had pulled up clean, so I turned on the camera phone for these lil' bops that were out there getting live, right? Then the nigga started pressing up on me and I had forgot that this bitch was still on."

Black gave a little chuckle, "You dumb ass nigga."

I smiled. "Fuck you, doe," was my come back. "Now check this out." I unclipped the phone from my necklace and handed it to Black.

Black started to watch the video. "Man, I know this hoe right here," he said, pointing at the screen. "Alright, I see you in the store now. Oh, *that* nigga. Yeah, that ole gang banging ass nigga," Black commented, as he continued to follow the recording. "Yeah, he bangs but he's for real with it, doe. Yeah, it looks like the nigga's trying to push up on something serious, Bleed." He got quiet and watched for a minute. "Man, Ta, you keep walking away, Man." He looked over at me. "If that was me I woulda__

I interrupted him. "Just keep watching, nigga."

*Bam! Baamm! Bam!* Black's eyebrows went up.

"Awww, hell naw! I know I ain't just see that! Hold up. Rewind this shit!" I reached over and restarted the video.

"Ha!" he said. "Haah! Man, you just put that boy down and peeled out."

Black was amazed by the video. "Man, now I remember how similar we are. That's why we hang out together." He looked over at me and shook his head. "Eh tap one, boy," he said. "I gots to see that shit one more time. I woulda did it just like that, Ta. I feel you. Too fly to fight tonight."

We laughed and clapped hands. We blazed up the water and you could see the little candle light flame when it got lit. Black was hugging my phone like a kid with a new video game.

"Eh Ta, here. You got a call coming through. Call from Felix," Black said.

"Oh hand me that. It's Felicia."

"Damn, man. Felix? That's a slick way of hiding some shit." He handed the phone over to me. "Why don't I think of shit like that? That's probably the reason why I'm always getting caught up by my baby's mother."

"Yeah, Ma," I spoke into the phone. "I'm on your street. You can start coming outside right now."

"Ta," Felicia said. "Don't you supposed to come to the door and walk me to the car?"

"Man, shiit Felicia. I thought that we was just kicking it to a party, Ma."

"Well, my father's sister is over here and she want to meet you."

"We ain't got time right now. Tell her I'll meet her tomorrow."

"See Ta, that's why I be acting like I do sometimes; 'cause you always got to be on that tough man shit."

"You know that we're pressed for time and we got to pick yo girl up too." I pulled up in her driveway.

"Saree is already over here. Don't you see her Jeep Wrangler in the driveway? Come to the door, Ta."

I got off the phone and just sat there for a minute. Man, she was talking 'bout coming to the door to meet her Auntie like we about to go to prom or something. This shit is starting to piss me off now. This broad is lightweight working me. Shiiit, the joke will be on me if I put in all this work and then another nigga knock her off at the set.

"Hold up, man. Tap something," I said to Black. "But don't light it up until I get back. Bet?"

"Alright. Bet."

"Hello," Felicia said. I had rang her back.

"Yeah, what's up? I'm at the door."

"Damn, you coulda at least rang the doorbell," she said.

"For what, Boo? We're on the phone right now."

She had a frustrated look on her face as she opened the door-but when she did I started to see why I was going through all this.

"Hey Ta," she said, with that soft, pretty voice.

"Don't hey me, Ma. Come here and give me a hug."

When she got close enough I stole a kiss. Auntie and Saree was standing off to the side giggling.

The Auntie said, "now that's a bold young nigga. Where's one of your uncles at Sugar?"

In a kinda shy way, I smiled. "I'll shoot him yo' number, and make sure that he calls you," I said.

Auntie continued drinking her Millers. "Oh boy, go ahead. I'm just messing with you."

"Ta, this is my Auntie Teresa. She wants to buy some weed to smoke."

Auntie cut in and said, "Yeah can I buy a sack, a holla, or whatever y'all call it?"

"Damn, I don't think that I brought nothing like that," I said. "Oh hold up, here you go, Auntie."

I reached into my pocket and gave her some of the weed that Black had gave me.

"Matter-of-fact, take this for free but I want you to call me and let me know how it is, alright?"

"Okay. Thanks, Sweety."

"What's up, Ta?" came a voice from the corner of the room.

"Oh shit, what's up, Saree?"

"You got some more of that for me?" she asked.

"Nope, but don't even trip 'cause Black got some for you and I think that he can't wait to see you."

# Chapter 6

Man, when I say that they looked good, I mean they looked good. Everybody came out sporting all black like GDs, but I swear we ain't plan it like that.

"Thanks Ta," Felicia said, leaning over and kissing me on the lips. Shiit, Black got caught with rubbers but never me because I'ma try to put a baby in this bitch no doubt.

"Is y'all ready?" I asked. I opened up the front door and we filed out. Once we got outside they looked at the whip in awe.

Then Saree said, "Damn, Ta. You out here killing 'em with that bitch."

"Wait to you see my nigga, Black's shit," I said, pumping up Black's status.

Black opened the door and lifted the seat up to let Saree get in the back. "What up, Black?" she said with her soft voice.

"Damn, what up Saree? Look at you, Ma. You all grown and shit, looking good. Long time no see." He was making Saree blush as he shot his game.

"Black, you know my girl, Felicia, right?"

"Naw, but I heard a lot about her," he said, pointing to me. "What the fuck did you do to my nigga, girl? He looked at Felicia.

That line always worked. I'm thinking to myself, '*good lookin' out Black.*'

Now you know when we get in there the plan is to be on some super Hollywood shit, 'cause that's what this set is about.

"Light up that stick, Mate," I said.

"For sure, Mate," Black replied.

The girls started laughing, then Felicia said, "Where is y'all niggas from? Australia or something?"

We both replied at the same time, "Yeah mate. You see the crocs mate?" We lifted our Mauri's in the air.

"Oops! I mean gators, Mate. Gator Dundee," I said.

Felicia said, "Stop playing. You is from 116th Street and Black, yo ass is from the projects."

"Ahhh! Is that right?" I was still playing with the fake accent. Then I pulled out the bottle of Rozay and said, "Here Ma. Pour yourself a drink and shut your bloody trap." Felicia punched me in the arm and started laughing.

We opened up the bottle and they filled their cups and they were surprised when we said that we were cool on the Rozay.

"I want to hit that," Saree said, pointing to the square that we was smoking.

"What, this water?"

"Hell yeah," she said, which was right up Black's alley. Black threw his hands up and said, "Fuck it. Let her hit it then."

When we pulled on the street where The Phase was located, we saw right away that that bitch was jammed packed. But the giggling in the back got our attention. Felicia turned around and said, "What is y'all watching back there?"

Saree started laughing, then said, "Girl, yo man is crazy."

"Let me see that." She reached back and grabbed the phone from them.

"Damn, man, how you get my phone, dude? And you still got that shit on?" I said, shaking my head with a mug on my face, talking to Black like I hadn't wanted the girls to see the video. *This nigga is infatuated with gun play.*

I really didn't want neither one of these chicks to see that because *you never know* who knows who.

"Hold up, Ta. This just happened?" Saree asked.

"Naw. No it didn't."

"Yes it did, Ta," she said. "I bet it was no more than about an hour ago." She pointed at the screen. "You still got on the same thing that you had on in this video."

The only thing good I could see coming out of this situation was that if girly in the back seat got something on her mind then she already knows what's gone come with the bullshit. Hot ones. "Ma, that ain't even real," I said, smiling.

"Yes it is, Ta. And who do you think you are?" Felicia asked.

Then she looked up from the phone and I saw her eyes look at the expensive dashboard, the bracelet and the chain I was wearing; then she looked in my face. I kept this nonchalant look, straight faced, almost a slight grin on my face. "Oh I see now," she said. "You is a nigga knee deep in the game, ain't you? I didn't realize it. This is all natural for you, huh?" She was smiling at me, looking down at the video still playing and then back up at me. She gave me this real sexy look like she was feeling me even more now. I gave her the same kinda smile.

*You have an incoming call from ...* I didn't let the computerized voice finish announcing who was on the line. Quick on the draw, I said, "let me get that. That might be some money." I grabbed the phone. I had forgotten that I was supposed to turn the phone off.

"Hello," I said into the phone. "Yeah, I'll be there in a minute. I'm 'bout to come around there right now." I hung up the phone and started the car. Pulling out I said, "Hey y'all, I gots to make one more stop before we go in." Everybody in the car was like, "Aww aw, Ta!"

"We already late," Felicia said. "Tell whoever that is that you'll come tomorrow."

"Hello." I dialed the number back. "As a matter-of-fact," I said, when they picked up, "I'ma have to get with you tomorrow. I just ran across some drama." I cut my eyes over to Felicia. "Naw, I can handle it really, doe. Alright. Alright. Peace." Then I turned the music back up and said, "Man, shut it." I looked at the two in the back seat and then at Felicia. "We 'bout to go in now, crybabies."

Man, our chicks was fine. Dressed in Dior and Prada with gladiator sandals on, to top shit off. They were the coldest things out this night and they knew it. I know niggas was thinking how could these niggas bring sand to the beach? Shiit, doe. If you was riding with who I was riding with, then you woulda seen how.

Even Saree was smiling in the back seat with Black, playing with his chain.

A nigga was feeling alright. I swear I was feeling cooler than a mothafuccka. And the way I felt, if the DJ played the right shit, like some Young Jeezy, some Lil Wayne, or even some of that old *Dipset* shit, yeah, definitely some of that, then I might just hit the floor like Johnny Gill.

Security guards and everybody else gave me a thumbs up and G-Nods for the old school classic. But really, I didn't know if they were complimenting me on the wheels or the chicks that we was with. Whatever, doe, I was like, "Let's go y'all 'cause we in here."

"Ten dolls at the door," said the big security guard with the S.M.G. logo on his shirt, standing for 'Self-Made Generals.' So I shot him eighty for all of us to get the nonchalant search so I can get the small thang in my girl's purse through.

I took a look around the place. *Yeah, I'm 'bout to go straight Hollywood in this bitch.* But first I thought, let me say what's up to all my niggas and the host of the party 'cause after the party then it's back to real life …

# Chapter 7

No kicking it. Just a simple dap and handshakes, then I'm back to kicking it with whom I came with.

Now see, this is my hood, and basically my job is to rep hard. So I'm showing who I came with how we get down.

*Okay. Let's make this quick*, I thought to myself. It's some action in here but I'm trying to get back to Felicia.

I walked around the party and made my presence be felt to my homies.

"What up?" I saw my nigga standing on the wall near the entrance.

"Ta, what up." Dap. Hug. Out.

"What up, Slick?" The next one of my homies I saw standing near the dance floor.

"Shiit, what up bohhy? I see you killing 'em," Slick said, dapping me up with one hand while holding a drink in his other hand.

"For sure, Slick. I see you killing 'em in here, too." Dap. Hug. Out.

Then I went down the whole bar dapping up niggas.

"What up, Trix?"

"Shiit, silking it."

"What up, J.T?"

"Shiit what up, Ta? I see that you found somebody for girly, huh?"

"Yeah. It's just a favor for my girl."

"Alright then, but tell her if her and dude don't work out then she can get at me."

"Bet," I said, dapping J.T. up before I moved on.

"Lo, what up?"

"Shiit, what's up, my little nigga? Here, my nigga. Take one of these drinks," Lo said in his own zone, passing me some Belvi.

"Bet." I took the drink, dapped him up, and stepped off.

"What up, Bo? What up, Key? What up, Gee? What up, Mike?" Dap. Dap. Dap. Dap.

"What up? Dill, Bill, Ron, D. Nail, Smooth and Killa Cas. What up?" Dap and out.

"Ro, what's going on with ya?" This was my nigga, Romell. He was the one throwing the set.

"What's happening, my nigga?" Ro was shining hard as usual. He had a face that smiles on G.P.

"I see you put this shit together again."

"Yeah. Hell yeah! This Jamaican chick that favors Jackie-O put everything together for me. I tried to change up a little this time, give it a different feel. You like, doe?" Ro asked.

"Yeah. Hell yeah, my nigga. I love it," I replied.

I can't even lie. They had the set looking right. I didn't even know where I was at for a minute. I shot to the bar on the other side and filled up the table with four bottles of Rozay and eight doubles of orange-cranberry and Belvi, plus four Coronas for the chasers.

I went back to the table to fuck with who I came with and the first thing that Felicia said was, "Ta, you got a lot of friends."

I wanted to say 'business partners' but I just left it at friends because we did all grow up together. And I ain't have to shoot one of these niggas yet. And they ain't had to shoot me. So I guess that's about as close to 'some friends' as you're gonna get in my hood.

"Yeah, but we don't hang out much, Ma. That's what I been trying to tell you." I moved closer to Felicia. "I only wants to fuck with you," I whispered to her. Felicia smacked her lips. "What's wrong, Bay?" I asked her.

"I don't know," she said. "It just looks like you got a fan club over there."

I looked to the next table and it was about four hoes over at the table beaning a nigga. I knew that I killed them with the Lacoste and the Levi game. "Ma, they looking at you," I said, trying to play it off.

Felicia's lips was so full and right that I just wanted to kiss her right there but I knew I couldn't do that 'cause *you never know* who's watching, who's getting paid to watch you or who's just plain ole haters.

"Ta, you're starting to make me feel a certain way," Felicia said, while she was twirling her straw in her drink.

"Straight up?"

'Yeah, Ta. I haven't felt like this in a minute."

"You haven't? So that means that you coming back to the spot with me, right?"

"I didn't say all that-but we'll talk about it." And right before the conversation was 'bout to get intense they started playing my shit. Record after record.

Cam'Ron's, *Get Em Daddy (Remix)*, then *Fireman,* by Lil Wayne, then 50 Cents, *Okay, You're Right*. And after smoking four dipped squares to the face plus with two drinks in yo hands, even Soldier Boy started sounding good.

Now we got our little breezies on the floor, you know, on some cool ass two stepping type shit. Niggas mean mugging from a far view, but that was the plan in the first place. After the real shit done took place, we 'pose to make as many people hate us or hate on us as possible. Why you think I brought the chain out? And the Mauri's, the shades, the black Barbie's and the henchman? To set shit all the way off. As CMB would say back in the days, 'we stunting all the way out.'

Big Luth had knocked him off something nice. That nigga, Slick looked like he was pulling out with something fly. And we were all in there having a good time. And I had told them everything about the set but one thing___that the bitch always, I mean always, end off with a fight. And right before I was about to tell them 'let's be out,' a Moet bottle came flying across the room, just missing us. Then another one came and hit the nigga right across from me dead in his shit.

Some St. Clair niggas ran over and stomped him out quick. Now two sets of niggas from two different hoods was fighting like crazy up in our shit. One nigga was over there looking like he was getting stomped to death so we knew we had to break the shit up. So we started pushing all of them niggas. Then they started firing shots and it was really time to hit the floor. "Hey, grab yo purse and tell them to come on," I said to Felicia.

"*Flaca, flaca, flaca.*"

We all got low and darted through the door. Black turned around and upped a hammer and let off a few shots of his own. I don't even know how he got that bitch up in there.

Damn. We got there at 12am. The set was 'pose to end at 4am, and it's only 1:30am. So we got into the whips and the funny thing was nobody was going nowhere. At least not until friendly rolled up, then all you heard was SCCUUUURRRED! Niggas peeling off asap.

"Is y'all alright?" I asked.

"Yeah, we cool," they all said together.

"Man, niggas is always fucking shit up," Saree said.

"Eh, y'all see that shit, doe? They was hating us in that *biotch*," I said

"Why was they hating? 'Cause I was with y'all?"

"Naw," I said. "Black explain to your girl what I mean."

"What he means is that they hated us 'cause we was the flyest thing in that bitch."

"And the more that they hate us, then the more we love it," me and Black said together, giving each other dap.

# Chapter 8

"That's right. Now tap something," I said in excitement.

"Say whaat!" Black said, feeding into my energy.

"Hell yeah, nigga. You heard. Dunk one, my nigga." I was referring to the water that we smoke. "This night ain't over unless y'all trying to go home?"

"I don't know, Ta. You and yo friends is wild."

"Felicia, that wasn't even my niggas that was scrapping, but since y'all acting like y'all sleepy, I'ma go head and drop y'all off, unless . . ."

Then they all was like "What?" I had them playing a guessing game.

"Unless..." I said, teasingly, "Y'all trying to go get something to eat?"

"Yeah, Ta," Felicia said. "Where we going?"

"Oh, I thought y'all was sleepy." Everybody laughed.

"Quit playing, Ta," she said. Then the phone rang, interrupting the laughing.

*'Call from Felix's house.'* They all looked at each other.

I answered. "Hello. Who? Oh. Oh what's up, Auntie Teresa."

"Ta, when can you bring me some more stuff?" she asked.

"Oh, like early tomorrow, Auntie."

"Yeah, I can say that was pretty much the best that I had in months," she said.

"Well, it's good to know that you liked it__ and we gone talk about it some more tomorrow, Auntie."

I hung up from Auntie and turned to look at the group.

"Man, where is y'all trying to eat at?" I asked.

"Let's eat at the Marriot since we gone be there anyway," Black said.

"Who said that we was going to the Marriot?" both of the girls said at the same time, smacking their lips

"Shiiit, I mean we still got some drinks and some more water to smoke, plus we already got the rooms, so what's really happening?" I said.

Felicia looked at Saree and they gave each other one of those girl to girl signs. "Okay I'll go, but I need some of that good Dro or some of that Kush 'cause it's a few things that I'm trying to get over," Saree said.

Black leaned over and whispered in her ear. I guess he was giving her some of the best consulting that he could because then he gave her an unexpected kiss. Then he pulled out the last bottle of Loud like he was doing a magic trick which made Saree smile, showing teeth. "Baby don't even worry about it. I got you, alright?" He handed Saree the sack and said, "This is for you and I'm 'bout to get you some cigarillos too, so you can roll up."

Felicia said, "I'm with the Telly but they food ain't all that, Mate."

I said, "Mate?"

"Yeah," she said. "You see the gator sandals. What y'all thought they were snakeskin?" She gave Saree a high five.

"Ahhh! That's what y'all on," I said.

"Hey, we can go to the Gyro House," Black said.

"I'm with that," Felicia said.

*Perfect choice*, I thought. Plus, that bitch is on the other side of town. I ain't trying to run into nobody that just left the party. The plan in my mind is to get this food and be out, straight hit the E-Way. Shiit, it ain't every day that you get to go to the telly with some chicks this cold.

When we pulled up, the girls told us to hurry up and let them out because they had to go to the bathroom.

"Here," I said, and handed Felicia fifty dollars. "I want cheese eggs with gyro meat and home fries. And get whatever y'all want, too."

Black ordered something similar and was about to go in with the girls, but I stopped him, "Eh, let me holla at you for a minute, Bleed," I said.

"Yeah, what's sup?"

"Yeah, I think we gone have to holla at your Arab dude tomorrow."

"Bet, Ta. You know that can go down."

"See, Black, you stays on yo one-two. And I respect that. So I'ma bless you if everything works out." I turned up the Belvi bottle and said, "but tonight, doe, I'm 'bout to bust this chick down and I ain't worried 'bout shit, you feel me?"

"I feel you, my nigga. I'm on the same shit."

"And look, if this move go through then you can consider us partners for life," I said.

"Man, I thought that we were already partners, Ta."

"Man, quit tripping, Black, 'cause you know and I know that we're just get high buddies. Mattera fact nigga, put one down right now before these chicks get back."

We clapped hands and lit one up for going to the top. "Right to the top" we said simultaneously.

"Damn, can we smoke too?" The girls came back from the restaurant with plastic bags. "Y'all just forgot about us, huh? And why is y'all smiling?" Felicia said.

"I ain't smiling, yet," I said, thinking about the episode that might go down.

The girls came out with a different swag, like they felt more comfortable with us. Truth of the matter was that I wasn't really that hungry, but I should be after I lose some of this protein. When Felicia got settled in her seat, she handed me a bottle of orange juice.

Saree said, "Black, do you like orange juice?"

"Yeah, I love it, Sweetheart."

"Sweetheart. Hah! Man, this nigga's tripping," I said, laughing so hard that I spit some of the drink out that I was sipping.

"Ta, shut up. It's good to be polite every now and then. So don't listen to him, Black," Felicia said.

"Man, I ain't studding that nigga."

"Hold on," I said, and put my drink in the cup holder. "And strap y'alls seatbelts 'cause I needs to rest this engine out."

I was on the freeway speeding with control like a NASCAR driver, passing cars. I had to swerve off from just missing a blue Camaro.

"Ta, could you slow down please?" Felicia said with an angry look on her face.

"Naw, my nigga. Punch that bitch," Black yelled from the back seat, egging me on.

*Veeeuwwwmmm!* We rolled right past the police doing about 100mph.

"Ta, ain't you gone stop?"

"Chill Felicia, we cool."

I peeped through the rear view and seen the gap that we had on them and instantly thought the hotel was only a few blocks up. So I hit the turbo switch and thought to myself that this might mess up everything, but fuck it.

I accelerated, *Veeeuuwwmmmm!* I shot across the exit then flew through the intersection. I made a hard turn into the hotel lot with no signs of friendly behind me. I took in a deep breath then looked at everybody with an embarrassed grin on my face. "My bad," I said.

Felicia snapped. "Ta, that's all you got to say is 'my bad?' You almost just got us killed."

Saree and Black was in the backseat sitting close together, hugged up, smiling, looking as if they had just went on a rollercoaster ride.

"Damn, Ma, I said, 'My bad.' I'm sorry, alright? Y'all good back there?" I asked.

"What the fuck is you tripping on?" Black asked. "You know we're alright. Matter-fact, let me out this bitch before friendly pull in here."

"Felicia?" I started to ask her if she was alright but she cut me off before I could finish my sentence.

"Don't Felicia me, Ta. You need to polish up. I'm a lady and you driving all crazy, boy."

Man, I'm starting thinking 'this might be a long night for me.'

# Chapter 9

I thought Ma was gone stay on some bullshit all night but soon as we got in the room she went to the bathroom and came out with nothing on but her panties and bra. Body sprays was smelling like oranges and peaches.

I couldn't take no more. I started kissing her dead in the mouth. I mean once you turn twenty-five years old, it ain't that many chicks that you can kiss. But being with her made me feel like we was back in high school again. That was cool with me, for real, 'cause a nigga was missing that type of shit lately. Yeah dawg, lately it ain't been no love in the city.

I got my hands on Felicia's fat ass while she held me tightly.

I slipped my tongue inside her mouth. Then I planted kisses on her neck and gently bit her ear. I unsnapped her bra, admiring her breasts as they sat up big and firm.

I grabbed them with both hands and sucked and kissed on them gently. "Ahhhhh, that feels so good, Ta," she whispered in my ear. I felt her move like chills were running through her body. Felicia's nipples were hard and her breasts were voluminous with light brown freckles.

I held them and kissed them in amazement, to the front of her nipples, to her neck, kissing and sucking them at the same time. I slid my hand down Felicia's perfectly slim stomach, letting my index finger and my middle finger caress her vagina.

Felicia arched her back in anticipation as I could feel how moist she was through her see-thru panties while massaging her pleasure box. Felicia screamed out, then came more soft moans, giving me an instant erection.

Pressing my body up against hers made her entire body become hot. Feeling my thick penis against her made Felicia open her legs wider as she was biting on my ear.

I took my shirt off and felt a rush. The combination of my blood flowing, mixed with the stimulation of the water, caused the muscles in my five-foot eleven frame to look more detailed. With nothing on but my Polo boxers, I slipped my tongue down the front of her neck in between her breasts, then slid it down, sucking on her navel.

"Ooooh Ta," Felicia said with her hands on my head. I slid her panties to the side exposing one side of her lips then started licking her misty vagina.

Felicia laid back with her eyes closed and after about thirty seconds of tasting and teasing, I pulled her panties all the way off, exposing her neatly shaved brownish lips and her pink slit in the middle of her thick long legs.

"Ahhh, ahh!" she screamed, as she came a second time from my tongue going to work. She sat up and moaned, then pushed me back and grabbed my stiff penis with both hands, feeling my pre-cum from anticipation. She opened her mouth and took my manhood into her mouth, returning the favor, which surprised me. It stimulated my body even more.

Felicia sucked and pulled out. She guided me into her wet vagina. I had one fist in the bed while the other one was helping me push myself in, looking like I was doing a one-handed push up. Finally, I pressed my penis against Felicia's vagina and rubbed it up and down before I pushed myself all the way in. Once I pushed in, she moaned, "Hit it hard, Ta," digging her nails into my back. The feel of her dripping wet lava turned me on even more. She was so moist that her juices began to overflow, soaking my abdomen and my balls, causing her own wetness to trickle down her crack.

*Smack, smack! Smack! Smack!* "Right there!" she screamed loudly, arms around my neck in a daze, clinching up from the pleasure and pain as she held on tighter with every thrust. "Oohhh!

Ta, don't stop! I'm cuming!" she screamed. Biting on my bottom lip, climaxing, she tightly wrapped her legs around my back.

After Felicia came she turned around and lay flat on her stomach, giving me a visual that made me even harder. Looking at her ass spread and her vagina sitting ready, I made two fists and put them into the bed with her waist in between them and proceeded to pump furiously. When I felt myself cuming I pumped harder.

*Clap! Clap! Clap! Clap!* Our skin hit.

"Ahhh!" I said as I sent a load deep inside her. She came a final time with tears of joy in her eyes, her face in the pillow. I fell on top of her from exhaustion.

I don't know if it was love in there, but it was definitely passion in the air. It's going down over here, and I just hoped that my nigga, Black, was having a time as good as mine. Breathing hard, I suddenly felt hungry. "Shiit," I mumbled to myself. "I'm 'bout to smash that gyro." I looked over at Felicia. "Then I'm gonna get round two in." But before I could get up the phone rang.

"Ta, who is calling you at three in the morning?" Felicia popped her head up off her pillow. "See, that's why I knew that I shouldn't did nothing with you. You probably got hoes jocking you left and right," she said.

But it was Will. "Chill, Ma. This my old school cat. He's like my uncle or something," I explained. "What's up Will?" I spoke into the phone.

"Ta, me and the Mrs. gots to head to the airport in a few hours. I don't want anybody going into the garage with me not being there. So if it's not a problem, I need you to keep the car until Sunday; if that's cool with you?" Will asked.

"Yeah, OG, that's cool with me."

"Alright then, good looking, Ta. And I'll see you Sunday."

"Oh, Will, hold up. Eh, say 'what's up' for me to my future wife here," I said, putting the call on speaker and holding it out so Felicia could hear. I wanted to let her know that it was really Will on the phone and not another female.

"Haa!" Will laughed and said, "Hello, how are you doing, Hun?" Then he told Felicia to make sure that she treat "his lil' man good."

"Alright," Felicia said. "But you better tell him to treat me good."

Will laughed and said, "He will. I'm sure of that."

"Okay," she said. "Nice talking to you, Uncle Will."

I took the phone off of speaker. "Alright Will," I said. "You be safe."

"Alright, you too, Loverboy. I'll see you Sunday."

The only reason that worked out is because I didn't have to rush out of the room in the morning. Other than that, I done shot a nigga and ran from the Po-Po in that bitch, so really, I was ready to give the whip back.

"Ta, if I was really your wife, how would I know that you'll come home to me every day?"

"Because Felicia, you'd be the only girl that I'll want to be with."

"Ta, not like that. I mean, don't you think that you need to calm down a little bit? See if you get killed then I won't have a future husband."

"Get killed? Ma, I ain't going nowhere. But if you want me to calm down, then I will. I'm on top of that asap. Anything for my sweetheart," I said, laughing at the inside joke. She laughed too.

"Stop playing so much, Ta."

"Naw, but for real, Ma, come here for a second."

"What?"

"I got to tell you something."

"Ta, what do you need to tell me?"

"You gotta be under the covers to hear me."

"Ta, you is caraaaazee!" she said, kissing me softly on the lips.

Round two. In love again and feeling good about it. No plans, just freedom sleeping in each other's arms.

"No, please don't come yet," Saree screamed. She put her long legs to use with her pretty feet on the bed in a squatting position, her hands on Black's chest, riding like a cowgirl.

"Ahhhh! Ooooo! AHHH!" Saree yelled, as Black grabbed hold of her just right sized breasts and watched them bounce up and down. Black was determined to last but Saree was riding so hard that he couldn't make a sound.

She started screaming louder as his hands cuffed both of her ass cheeks, giving her a boost which made her pound harder on him every time she came down. Her oiled up ass was smacking Black's thighs.

Then she reversed her position, turning around with her knees in the bed, still riding. Her position allowed Black to see Saree's heart shaped ass along with her vagina that was so wet that the hairs around it, they looked so silky that you'd think they were permed. Saree grabbed Black's shins and continued to ride. He moved his hands from her ass to around her waist, lifting when she went up and pulling down hard when she came down.

*Smack! Boonk! Smack. Boonk!* As they were going at it in the heat of passion, the head board of the bed repeatedly banged the wall. After ten more seconds, Saree came down and Black held her down as they climaxed together.

# Chapter 10

I had a dream that I was sitting on top of a stack of money about eight feet high and about as wide as bunk beds. Black was in it too.

"Black, what up, bohhy!"

"Ta, what's up with you?"

Then I said, "Black, look at all this money we sitting on, Bohhy!"

"I know, bohhy, right?" Black said.

"Right!" I answered back.

Then I ended with my head in the air and a Rick Flair 'Whoooo!'

I woke up about eleven; housekeeping knocking on the door.

I jumped up quick and grabbed my pants. "Hey Felicia, here you go," I said and handed her about eleven hundred dollars. Her eyes got big.

"Ta, what I'm supposed to do with this?" she asked.

"I don't know. Get the room for another day. And y'all can go shopping or something. And look," I said, "all these stores around here. Plus y'all can rent a car until we come back. I got a few runs to make."

"What is you about to do, Ta?"

"I'm trying to put together a retirement plan."

I called Black. "Hey nigga, is you ready, man? I know you ain't still hugged up. Snap out of that shit."

For real, yesterday was a masterpiece in my eyes, but you don't have days like that sitting around. You know niggas ain't inheriting no big dollars, so if we want some more of those nights then we gone have to stay grinding.

"Alright, I'm up," he said, his voice still hoarse. "Let me brush my teeth and I'm out there. Oh yeah, Ta. What about girly?"

"Yeah, they cool. They gone rent the rooms again and go shopping and shit like that. Don't worry. Just hurry up. Oh yeah, and call yo' dude. You think that he's up?" Spitting toothpaste in the toilet, my words came out mumbled.

"He should be," Black said. "In fact I'm 'bout to hit 'em up in a second."

We were ready to go in no time. Black jumped in the whip and pointed towards the street while he was talking on the phone; with a nod at me, saying that 'everything was everything.'

"Where we got to meet dude at?" I asked. But he ignored me.

He was on the phone chopping it with his Arab dude like, "Man, whatever, O. We lil' niggas, huh? Omni, I got one question for you. How much of your own shit you been smoking?"

My nigga had a gift to gab that I admired. But I was anxious to show O that we could hold our own. As the quality and the quantity was good, we was all the way together.

Black looked over at me and said, "Alright, go on Lakeshore," which was cool because that's close to where I had to go to get the paper from on St. Clair. We made my stop first. I went into the house and grabbed the whole $29,000 that I had in there and threw it into a bowling bag. If somebody was gonna rob me then they better do it now, 'cause that was everything from the duck off spot, over here anyways.

I jumped back in the whip and shot straight to the store that O said meet him at.

"Pull up right here," Black said, pointing to a spot right in front of the store.

"You let this nigga know that we got straps, right?"

"Man, be cool, Ta. This dude sells straps, alright? Man, believe me when I say this dude is alright with me. Plus he's good business," Black said. We got out of the car and walked into the store.

"Eh, give me a pack of Newport's and that's it," Black said. Then he seen the guy we came in to see and he was like, "O, what's up, bohhy?"

"Eh, what's up, Black?" O gave him some dap and a hug, showing each other some hood love.

O looked at me, then told Black to tell your dude to loosen up. He was referring to me, but I wasn't tense at all.

We went through four doors and then walked down some stairs to the basement.

"Yeah, O__, so this is my man, Ta, right here. He's my business partner."

"Ta, what's up?" said O, extending his hand to me.

"What up, O?" I shook his hand business style.

Then O went on saying, "I heard some good things about you, Ta." He pulled a half a blunt out of his cigarette box, sparked it up, took a drag and then ashed it.

"So what are you guys trying to do? One or two? If it's two then I'll let them both go for, uhm, twenty-eight hundred," O said. "That's only 'cause you're friends with my man."

I looked at Black and we both started laughing at what O had said. O said, "What?" He acted like he was being insulted. "That's a deal, man," he said, still pulling on his blunt. "That's the best price that I can give you," O added. "Eh man, ask yo friend what's so fucking funny."

"Naw, it ain't no disrespect, O. "It's just that my partner was trying to spend a little more than twenty-eight hundred."

O said, "Okay then, I'll give you five for $5,500 and that's my final offer."

"O, let us get twenty for $29,000 'cause that's all that I got to offer," I said, sitting the bowling ball bag on the table.

"Oh, you guys are for real, huh?"

"Man, what you thought, we were toddlers or something?" I said.

"I like this guy," said O. Then he said, "I can do that, but first both of you is gonna have to take yo' shirts off."

"Man, take our shirts off? Man, it ain't no friendly over here, my nigga." I blew up, not liking O's suspicion towards us.

"No offense but you can keep your money," said O, with a heartbroken type of face. "Eh Black, tell this guy where we met at."

"Me and O met in the county, Ta. A nigga that he treated like family tried to set him up. He beat the case but he still don't trust anybody to this day. Man, just take your shirt off, Ta."

"Alright, but I'm not putting my strap down."

"That's fine with me; but I do real business. And if I wanted you robbed I would have been did it. But see, my friend, to me all business is big business, you see?" He pointed and when we looked over, O had four of his dudes in the back strapped up with AKs ready to go. This dude was making me nervous, doe; smoking weed and shit and smiling with bloodshot eyes like everything was a game.

"Hahpee," he said. Then he spoke some shit that I couldn't understand but they came back with brown bags like the ones they used in the store.

It was twenty pounds in four bags. Barely five pounds in each bag. He put a pound from each bag on the scale and they all came up to 448 pounds.

His dudes counted the paper then hit him with a thumb's up.

"It's all there, boss," said one of the workers.

O dapped Black up and gave him a hug. I gave him a nod on my way walking out, but I started to feel like I was being disrespectful so I turned around and gave him an enclosed handshake also.

I bought an Arizona and went and put that tree in the trunk.

O followed us out, took a look at the Cutty and said "Nice wheels."

"Good looking," I said, looking at O's Hummer. "Yours ain't too bad either."

We pulled out, but bohhy, if Will only knew what type of shit I was doing in his whip he would probably kill me no doubt.

# Chapter 11

"Ta, how you feel about O?" Black was smoking on a Newport going through the CDs when he asked that question.

"Man, dude alright, I guess. I ain't really feel that take my shirt off shit, doe."

"Man, Ta, you be thinking that this shit is all about you sometimes," said Black, shaking his head with a disgusting scowl on his face. "Man, that dude is married with two kids. And he got an establishment to run. Plus he almost got locked up for ten years 'cause somebody that he thought was close to him tried to set him up. Ta, Man, I hate to say it, but sometimes you be on some selfish and disrespectful type shit, and if we're gonna be partners then that's one thing that I won't tolerate."

*'This nigga ain't have to spend a dime and talking 'bout what he won't tolerate,'* I thought.

"For real, Ta. Man, look…, you ain't even thank a nigga for the plug. Man, just imagine the flip," Black said.

"Man, I'm hip to the flip as long as the product's good."

"Good? What don't you understand about us having the plug?"

"Man, you got the plug!" I replied.

"Naw, Nigga, we got the plug. And all you had to do was take off yo' punk ass shirt just so he'll know that you was solid. Eh, and if young'un act like that, then I ain't even trying to be involved," Black said.

Now I knew and he knew, that if you want to buy in this game then the connect is just as important as the money. So, therefore, I'ma fuck with his nigga a few more times then I'm out this bitch.

"Man, shut up with all that crying, dude. You already know that I'ma handle my part. Shiit. I told you that if this shit pop then we're partners for life. So how do you want to do this shit?" I asked.

I knew Black, and he was pretty much just like me. So I basically already knew the answer to that question.

"We can dump these bitches *or* we can get all the way on our dirty."

"That was sacks and bottles. So that way we're shooting for somewhere around two hundred thousand dollars instead of one hundred thousand. So, now we just gotta find the spots that we gone grind at."

"So when do we start?" Black asked, looking anxious like he was already ready to go.

"Shiit, basically tonight. We post up outside at the clubs, bars, and after hour spots, but we do nothing today. Tonight, doe, we post up outside and sell everything for five dollars cheaper and a few grams bigger than everybody else's. This is how we kill the game, doe. And we gotta do it quick because that way we're gonna be stepping on everybody's toes. The way I see it, if we make 600 an ounce with sixteen of those in every pound, we should come out somewhere around two hundred thousand. And coming from twenty nine thousand, that sounds like a hellified flip.

"Eh, what's up, Boo? I grabbed you some white peach Abboccato wine," I said. Me and Black were making our way back to the hotel and I was giving Felicia a heads up.

"Thanks, Bay. Hey they got some nice stuff around here. This pizza I got comes straight from an Italian restaurant and if y'all don't hurry up it's gone be cold."

"We headed there right now. Y'all already up there, right?"

"We're on our way."

"Ahhh! You rushing me and y'all ain't even there yet? Alright Ma, we headed right up there. Matter fact, I'm 'bout to change my clothes then we'll be there."

Saree was in the back ground yelling, "Tell Black that I miss him."

"Eh, Black, Saree said that she misses you." I told him and chuckled. "Man, hold up," I said into the phone. "That man got a phone. She gone have to pay me for all these extracurricular activities," I said and glanced at Black. "Look this nigga over here smiling like a motha. And not just smiling, he over here cheesing, Boo. Alright, Felicia, let me handle this and I'll see you in a minute."

"Bye Ta," she said, as we ended the call.


I stopped by my place to pick up some clothes. I didn't want to look all thuggy, but at the same time I needed to look like I was about business. So I got my Polo boots and grabbed a thin hoody and a pair of Roc-Jeans Classics, you know, something a little more comfortable to hustle in.

We swung by Black's next. He came back out with Polo Joggers – all black. And he wore an all-black Indians fitted. He actually wore all black a lot. Besides his complexion I guess that's where he picked up his name from.

We got back to the telly and the girls was both in my room. Saree was just finishing a half a blunt that she had from the night before. They had rented a new Honda Accord and they were wearing leggings with characters from different cartoons on them. For us to be grown-ups, I still thought that they were incredibly sexy.

Felicia was twenty-two years old and she had already finished up four years of college. Plus, she didn't have any kids yet. Her father was a stone cold hustler who had owned restaurants and a corner store, so the street mentality was in her already because of that. She lived in the suburbs but she would always be at her grandma's house so you never knew. I mean, always.

"What's up, Boo?" I said. "Here's the wine I was telling you about." I handed Felicia the bottle after giving her a kiss on the lips.

"Thanks, Boo." She smiled at me. "Saree get some cups."

"Eh, where that pizza at?" Black said.

"It's on the counter, but y'all ain't even washed y'all hands yet."

"Naw, Bay, it's cool," I said, smiling at Black. "We got some of that hand sanitizer stuff." We both rushed towards the pizza."

"Look, it's still early, so tonight I want you to do what you want to do." I was talking with food stuffed in my mouth. "Here go five dollars. I looked over at Black so he could follow my lead. "See me and old buddy gots to handle a few things."

"Some more business?" Felicia said, with her hand on her hip, shifted to one side.

"Yeah, some more business, but look, since y'all driving, meet us at The Tonight Palace Bar, downstairs," I said.

"Soo, since y'all leaving then I guess y'all won't be able to see us in these," Felicia said, pulling out her Chanel swimming suit, swinging it from left to right.

"Shiiit, I just told y'all that we was gone be here for a couple of more hours."

"Hey, we going to the pool, slow pokes," the girls said. "Catch us if y'all can!"

"Hold up. Shiit. We coming," me and Black said with grins on our faces.

# Chapter 12

After a few hours of dunking and splashing our females it was time for us to be out. I was gone tell Black that we wasn't gonna smoke no more water on this grind. I had a whole ounce bottle left and if he wanted to smoke with me then that was on him. If not, doe, more for me.

I already had the plan to see if most niggas that was pushing bottles, sacks and ounces would buy pounds from me. So what I'd planned on doing was to tell everybody that I ain't got shit. Then when niggas start feeling like they're going on a diet, that's when I'll tell them, 'look, my little nigga, B, got something but he's only selling dime, quarters and ounces.' That way we'll reach that number that we're trying to hit and could get back to O quick.

"Hello. What's up, Luth?" My nigga, Big Luth was the first one I called. "Nope. Shiiit, it's still dry out here, Luth. But look, my nigga, B, got something but he's only working with ounces."

Bring 'em through? Alright. Be there in a minute." Yeah, my plan was going to work.

Part B of the plan: I'd pull up in the gas station and wait until a pack of niggas or bitches pulled up and go into the store. Then I'd go in after them. I'd cop a box of Swishers like I was about to smoke. Then I'd sit in the car, roll one up, and just let it burn like incense. They'd smell it, then want to inhale it. Shiiit, we had some Loud that was better than the average Dro. One look and a real weed smoker a jump right on it.

Then I'd tell them, "Man, I'ma just sell you something out of my personal sack." That was one of my favorite lines. "That way ya'll can keep the jack boys off yo' back, because it don't look like you're doing that much. Just getting high, you feel me?"

Yeah, I can just picture how the conversation would go.

*"Hello. I know that I was 'pose to show up earlier, but you must haven't read the paper. Shiiit, I ain't even got time to tell you what happened, but let's just say it ain't looking good for the home team."*

*"Man, you ain't got nothing, Ta?"*

*"Zilch," I said in my best hustlas voice. But since you one of my cats, I can hook you up with my lil' man's, but all he got is ounces. That's cool? Alright, then I'll be right there.*

Me and Black were on a roll. But before we started out on our plan, I had to be sure to keep my promise of more weed for Felicia's aunt. After a stop or two, I drove to Felicia's house. Leaving Black in the car, I walked in and handed Auntie Teresa a Corona that I had bought from the store.

"So what's up, Auntie?"

"I want something for eighty," Auntie said, which was only four blunts, but I stretched it out. Plus, Auntie smokes joints anyway, so she's good.

Then she pulled out a piece of paper with about seven people's names on it.

She said, "okay, Junior wants two ounces, Dawn said she wants an eighth of an ounce, Stephany says she wants something for twenty, Ronald from around the corner said that he wants to spend one hundred, Sherry's got fifty dollars to spend, and Lil' Dante from upstairs said can he buy a holler."

"Auntie," I said, and shook my head, "run that back for me real quick 'cause if they want it I got it." And I was gonna make sure that they was gone get it.

Auntie gave me the sheet, then gave me a kiss on the cheek. "Ta, do you know where I can get some of that other stuff at?" Auntie asked.

"Not off hand," I said. "But if I find some, I'll let you know. And if you want, you can give your peoples my number, Auntie, and I'll look out for you."

"Okay, Sweety. And when you talk to my niece tell her she needs to call her father."

Black's little cousin had called while I was inside saying that he was at Peabody's. They was about to do a show there and him and about ten other performers up there needed some trees asap. We were on a roll.

That Saturday night we met back up with the girls at The Tonight's Palace after we stashed the weed and money. Man, in a four and half hour span we managed to make $13,000. In one day, we'd made half of the money that we spent to buy it.

"What's up? Where is ya'll at?" Felicia called my phone as we were pulling up in the parking lot.

"Behind y'all," I replied.

Felicia looked around but didn't see the Cutty because I had switched up.

"Ta, stop playing so much. And if you're behind me then what do we got on?"

"I don't know, but I see four nigga's, two with Indian's fitted on sitting on their cars. One nigga just tried to grab your hand."

"Oooh! They are back," Felicia said, laughing. She and Saree then tried to rush away from the dudes that was trying to holla at them.

She didn't notice the forest green Porsche truck. The Cutty was too hot to keep riding on the grind, especially to ride back to the telly in.

"Eh, tell them niggas to beat it, Ma. And order me an orange-cranberry and Goose."

"Okay. And Black said he wanted some what? This nigga want some Jack. Man, I tell you, this nigga here is a cowboy. With Pepsi. Oh, that makes it better," I said in a sarcastic way but thinking, *this dude need to mellow out.*

"Ta, man, you couldn't pick a better bar then this one?" Black said, looking irritated.

"Man, what's wrong with this one? They play some nice music, plus it's right off the freeway to where we're headed."

"Yeah, but I can't get the strap in there," he complained.

"Black, leave it under the seat."

"Man, what if something jumps off?"

"Man, look, we're about to go in here and have a few drinks and then we back to the telly, that's it."

We stayed in the bar for about ninety minutes eating Buffalo wings and drinking. The four of us started to engage in some serious conversation. And the drunker we got, the more we debated.

Felicia – *"Jehovah Witnesses, 'cause who else is gone come to your door just to prove a point and talk about their god?"* . . . Black – *"Man, I can't lie, Biggy was that nigga for real. But Pac was colder than that nigga hands down"* . . . Saree – *"Man, that dude should get the chair for all that shit that he did." "What?"* we all said.

*"Well, he should get lethal injection. Ya'll knew what I was talking 'bout. And I woulda never thought that Cleveland would have a black serial killer."*

Ta – *"Hank Aaron wasn't the first black Major League player. It was, uhm, damn, I can't think of his name right now but I know that it wasn't Hank Aaron"*. . . Saree – *Jazz is relaxing, but I prefer R & B. Now that's my favorite kind of music. It's really incomparable"* . . . Felicia – *"I know for a fact that he play more roles than anybody. I counted twenty movies that he played in off-hand without even really thinking about it."* Black – *"I ain't even into that. Hell naw, not at all. In fact I'm actually offended that you'll even ask me some shit like that"* . . .

"Damn! Shut up, Black," Saree said, laughing at him. "Don't get defensive about a little question."

*"Man, I swear the one sister is better than the other one,"* I said, continuing with our rambling conversations. *"It don't matter, doe, 'cause they body be getting that gwaala!"*

"Why is them niggas still looking over here?" Felicia asked while rolling her eyes at them.

"I don't know, but I ain't see the niggas holla at one bitch since we been here," Black said.

"They must have just got through doing a stretch in the joint," I said, laughing. Me and Black got a kick out of my joke.

"Shhhh! Ta, be quiet. They might of heard that." Felicia was looking concerned, trying to keep the drama down.

"Man, fuck them niggas and what they heard," I said. "And I don't remember being an entertainer so what the fuck is y'all looking at!"

"Black, please get him," Felicia pleaded. "And let's go."

"Naw, my dude," said one of the hustlas. "It ain't like that. We was just trying to find some weed and we ain't from round here."

"So what's wrong with you finding some?" I asked, looking at dude with a stiff grill.

"We're from Toledo, my dude, and like I said, I just needed somebody to point me in the right direction. But don't worry 'bout it, it's cool, man. I don't want no trouble either."

"Okay. Look, man, what is y'all trying to do? All I got is ounces of Loud, and they go for six hundred apiece."

"Can I check one out?"

"Yeah, but, my nigga, I ain't got no scale on me, so if you want it, you want it."

"It's cool," said dude, "cause we got one in the car."

I waived at my peeps telling them to go on to the truck. I gave the keys to Black and told him to watch his back.

We had put all of the weed up, but had kept a quarter pound just in case something like this jumped off. On the ruler, what we had read was twenty-nine grams.

"What's up my dude?" I said. "This really ain't no good area for this kinda activity." I kept my eyes peeled for friendly and watched the out of towners at the same time.

"Yeah, let me get two of them ounces," dude finally decided.

He went to two of his dudes and they all pieced up on $1,200 real quick and shot it to me.

"Bleed, what's up? Can I contact you?" I shot him a number to the other phone. "What's yo name?"

I gave him an alias and said, "they call me P.Air. What's yo name, dude?"

The stranger replied, "Elijah when I call-but just call me Eli."

I jumped in the whip and thought to myself $14,200. What a night. We out here."

"Hello," the nurse at the front desk said, answering the phone.

"Umm, yeah. Can I get Room 214?"

"Who would you like to speak to?" she asked.

"Rico Davis, ma'am."

"Yes, could you please leave a name and number? The patient can't receive calls this late."

"Alright. Just tell him that his cousin Elijah called to check on him. He should already know the number. Thanks."

## Chapter 13

The girls beat us back to the telly. Me and Black had decided that we wasn't going to do too much on Sunday since it was gonna be our last night at the hotel.

"Man, I ain't been home in two days and I ain't been answering my BMs calls either," Black said.

"Man, you better call her before she start thinking you dead or something, my nig. 'Cause one thing we don't need is friendly in our mix," I said as he was putting the rest of the money up.

"Eh, do you know that we made fourteen thousand dollars tonight? Is that championship shit or what?"

"Yeah," replied Black, but the words came out in a depressed state.

"Yeah damn, man, what's on your mind, Bleed?" I said to Black. "It looks like something is bothering you."

"Yeah, it is. It's Saree."

"Saree?" I was confused and said, "I thought you liked Saree."

"Shiit, like her? I love her. But what do I supposed to do about Tona and my seeds? Look, all Tona do is bitch and tell me how I ain't never gone be shit. And the two nights that I just had with Saree, I done had more fun than I had in my whole twenty-five years of living. Man, I shouldn't be telling you this," Black said, after taking a deep breath.

"Naw, go ahead. It's cool, my nigga," I said.

"I don't know. Me and girly been talking 'bout getting a spot together or really she just want me to move in with her at her spot. I don't' know, doe. I'm still undecided with that."

"Alright, look. Since you're my little nigga this what I want you to do. First call yo babies mamma and let her know that you're good. And tomorrow when you get up, we can work on getting you your own duck off. A solo crib first and then you can make your decisions from there."

"We supposed to be stacking dough, Ta."

"Look, don't worry 'bout that 'cause we gone make dough. Just make sure that you call Tona 'cause we don't need no heat. You feel me?"

"Alright, Ta. But let me ask you a question."

"Ask me anything."

"Alright then…how do you feel about Felicia?"

"Bohhy, if I told you, then I might have to kill ya." I was joking for a second, but got serious. "Naw, put it like this: I'ma have to take care of my seed because I only got one girl right now. You feel where I'm coming from? Man, we got a goal to reach and we gone do it, right?"

"Right," he replied. It seemed like his spirits were back up.

"P.F.L., my nigga. Partners for Life, right?"

"Man__ that shit sound corny, Ta."

"Whatever," I said. "Here smoke this, and I'ma smoke this, and I'm about to go get my money's worth out this bitch 'cause we out of here tomorrow, right?"

"Right."

The rest of the night I sat back with Felicia and watched repeats of Martin clowning off some of my favorite episodes.

This was the last night at the telly but we were discussing when we was going to see one another again, and the results was soon and a lot.

The summer was about to start in two weeks and she'd be out of school until her fall classes started. She told me that if I kept acting crazy, then she was going to cut the relationship short no matter how much she loved me. Shiiit, really? I thought I was kind of mild compared to the rest of my niggas that I came up with.

"Ta, promise me that you'll stop acting so wild."

"Ma, I promise, but really__

"Really what?" Felicia asked, cutting me off.

"I mean, I really love you and will do anything it takes for me to keep you," I said, crossing my eyes trying to make her laugh.

"Ta, you are so phony," she said, laughing hard.

"Naw, I'm for real, Ma," I said, smiling."

In a way I was for real, but I couldn't see what she meant by saying I was wild. See, one thing that I learned coming up was to always protect your family, your money and your woman. And my Uncle Keith always told me to take death before dishonor. And that's what I thought that I was doing. I figured that little Ma was just a little over protective. And in a way I kinda thought that was cool because the love line was thin over here.

"Oh Felicia, why didn't you call your Auntie and let her know that you was cool." I changed the subject. "Plus she said your father was trying to get up with you."

"Boy, my Auntie got my number. If she was that worried she would have called me. And if you ain't noticed, Auntie is kinda messed up."

I laughed. "Kinda?" I said.

Felicia looked at me and smiled. She said, "Naw. She is thahroooo! She good peoples, doe."

"True dat," I said. "Yeah, and she probably get a check too." We both chuckled.

But you know tomorrow's my day off, and Monday it's back to business. And with this connect-I'm thinking about a retirement plan for real. Plus, I'm thinking wedding ring for my breezy next to me.

"Ta, can we do something simple together tomorrow?"

"Simple like what? Go to McDonalds?" I said, laughing.

"Yeah, that a be cool," Felicia said, with a straight face.

"Wow. This shit just keep getting better and better," I said, shaking my head. It was hard to believe that someone as fine as

Felicia would want to just go to McDonalds. "Yeah, we can do that and you gone order happy meal, right?"

"Bohhy stop. I can eat a whole quarter pounder meal."

"Yeah? Okay, we'll see"

Tona ended up calling Black one hundred times while he was sleep. Saree got tired of the phone ringing and answered it since he didn't. They were on the phone arguing back and forth. Tona ended up calling my baby's mamma and telling her that we was somewhere tricking with some prostitutes. How I got into it, I don't know. Then, my BM started texting me, talking 'bout 'I'll see you in child support court, bitch.' Felicia got mad and wanted to fight with my BM. And this nigga, Black, was looking so confused that it was pathetic. Tona claimed that she had burned all of his clothes.

"Shiiit," Saree said. "That was cool because he wasn't going back there anyway."

Drama on top of drama. Man, I gots to make sure that this nigga got his head on straight 'cause for real, we still gotta lot of tree to move. And in the middle of everything, my phone rang.

"Hello," I said. "Yeah Slick, what's up?"

"Shiit, silking it. What's up with you, bohhy?"

He was just the nigga I needed to talk to. "Eh Slick, I need to rent out one of yo' spots asap. Tell me you still got one."

"Man, I don't got no two families left, Ta. And I know that you probably trying to put one of yo lil breezys in there, right?"

"Sorta, but not really, doe. It's not a female at all. Friend of the family, my nigga."

"Oh yeah, I got a single family over on the south side."

"What you want for it?"

"Man, everything in it is new. New carpet and it's already furnished."

"Man," I said, "I'll take it. How much?"

"For you, give me six hundred a month plus first month's deposit, and that will be twelve hundred all together. And really that's two dollars less than I was gone charge my other nigga," he said. "And whoever gonna be there, just tell them to stay low and keep it plain, ya dig."

"Bet. I got you, Slick," I said. "And I'll link up with you in a couple of hours."

*Man, this nigga, Black, better be happy*, I thought. And this nigga gone have to stay on his shit. Shiiit, we set a goal and I ain't stopping until we hit that number.

# Chapter 14

"Hello."

"Yeah, hello."

"What's up?" Rico said.

"Yeah, Rico. What it do, my nigga?"

"Not much. Who dis?"

"This Eli, bohhy. How you feel, homie?"

"I'm stable, so they telling me, my nigga," he replied.

"That's love, my nigga," Eli said. "Check this out, doe, right? You know that bitch ass nigga, Ta? The one that pulled that stunt on you, right?"

"Why wouldn't I know the nigga? That's the nigga I plan on taking out as soon as I get released from here," Rico said, clinching his teeth reliving the incident for a split second.

"Right, doe, but look," Eli said. "You just sit back and I'ma handle that shit. See, I came across the nigga yesterday and I guess that he ain't remember me from being at the store, but check this out. I got the nigga's number and everything."

"Yeah?" Rico asked, as he lifted up and focused more on what Eli was talking about.

"Yeah," Eli said.

"Man, you shoulda waked that nigga right there."

"Naw chill, my nig, 'cause look, it was too many people around at the time. But I'ma kill two birds with one stone," Eli said. "Cause see, the nigga got some Loud weed that he's selling with that east side nigga that they call Black."

"Oh yeah, I'm hip to that rowdy ass nigga," Rico said.

"Yeah, so I'ma set these niggas up real swell, so don't worry about shit. I got these niggas on my radar."

"Straight up?" Rico said.

"Yeah, straight up, Cuz. No bullshit. Yeah, so you can consider this nigga through."

"Through?" Rico said.

"Yeah, through," Eli said, laughing, loving the idea of whacking Ta. "It's over with," Eli said. "So get some rest, man, and I'll see you in a minute."

After we left the hotel we followed the girls to the rental place to drop off their car. For some reason we planned on not grinding on Sunday. Probably because we promised the girls that we was going to spend the whole weekend with them.

"Eh, Black, what's the move?" I asked.

"Oh yeah, drop us off at girly's Jeep. We're about to catch a movie downtown. Then I'll link back up with you in a minute," he said.

"Oh yeah, that reminds me. You gotta come with me to check this spot out," I said.

"Oh, you got a new spot?" he asked.

"Not for me. *For you*, dumb nigga. Yeah, bohhy, what I tell you last night? That was my word."

"Man, you already paid for it?"

"Why Blizzy?" I said.

"Because Ta, I already told you that I might move in with Saree."

Man, a nigga can't move on "mights" now days. Now, if he woulda said for sure then I would've let that shit ride. But for this grind that we're about to be on, everything gotta be for sure.

"Man, do you really think that would be a good move?" I asked.

"What you mean?"

"I mean you don't even know for sure, and you just met this girl. Not to be taking anything away from y'all chemistry, but do you think moving in with her is really gone sit right?" I paused for a second. "Man, listen," I continued. "I can't have you going out on me. No baby mamma drama and no unexpected D.V.s. See, we're on a mission for this paper and that's why I need you to keep yo' head level."

"Man, how much is it gone be a month, Ta?"

"Six hundred dollars a month. But don't worry 'bout it 'cause the first month is on me. But it's definitely coming out of your percentage."

"First month and deposit would be twelve hundred, right?'

"Right," I said.

"Twelve hundred, huh? Well, here go twelve hundred right here." He pulled out a bundle of bills. "Cause you're absolutely right, partner. It's time for me to grow up," Black said.

I started smiling and said, "Whoa! This boy is playing with some *dineros*. You sure about this, right? 'Cause you know I'll love to take it out of yo' percentage and add interest, if necessary."

"Man, take this damn money before I change my mind." He pushed the money in my chest. "Oh yeah, here go two hundred dollars, too."

"What's this for?" I asked.

"That's for the next bottle of water we cop."

"Eh, you know once twelve o'clock hit that it ain't Sunday no more," I said.

"Right, right," Black said, with a smirk on his face. We were both on the same page ready to get it in. "Man, what's taking these broads so long?"

"Eh, man, why you call my bitch a broad?" I said.

"Man, you is crazy," Black said. "And here they come right now. I bet you five hundred dollars that you won't call Felicia a bitch when they get in the car." My eyes lit up.

"Bet," I said.

Black copped deuces, changing his mind, and said, "naw, yo crazy ass a probably do that shit."

"What's so funny? Why y'all laughing?" Felicia said.

Then Saree said, "I know__. Can y'all fill us in on the joke?" Then my other phone rung. My whole facial expression changed when I heard the voice. My smile had instantly turned into a frown. I tried to steady my voice. I remembered that I had seen this nigga the night I shot Rico. But business is business and if he want to do business—

"Yeah hello," I said.

"Yeah P.Air? What's up? This is Eli."

I said, "What's up?" then held my finger up in front of everybody because I needed them to be quiet.

"Yeah, this is Eli from last night," he said.

I already knew who it was because no one else would have called me that. That's the type of shit you do when you don't trust a nigga but can't pin the reason. "Oh what's up, my man?" I said. "Yeah, what up, Eli?"

"Yeah homie, I'm trying to link up with you. Do you think we can bump heads in traffic?"

"Damn, man, you know what? My hands is all tied up right now. But I should be coming out later on," I said.

"Okay. That a work," Eli said. We ended the call but I didn't say nothing for a minute.

"Ta, who was that?" Felicia asked. It was easy for me to tell that she wasn't asking out of jealousy, but she caught the bad vibe.

"Oh nobody really," I said.

'*Cause that's what dude is gone be if he keeps fucking with me. Nobody,*' I thought to myself.

Eli was talking to one of his boys. "That lame, Ta, talking 'bout his hand is tied up right now," he said. "Yeah, that ain't gone be the only thing tied up when I'm through with this nigga, ya dig?"

# Chapter 15

Yeah, these are the type of days that I can do without. First, I got to drop Black and Saree off at Felicia's house so they can get her Jeep. Then go to Micky D's and take a walk in the park with my lady. Then go back to Felicia's house. Then switch cars and pick up some product and come back.

Then I have to drive back across town to meet up with Slick; come back and bring Black to his new spot; put some money in my baby's mother's mailbox to keep her cool; wait for Will to call so I can drop off his wheels. Then I gotta catch the damn water man before it gets too late and he gets off the scene. Oh, and I can't forget that I gots to listen to the radio all day and night just to find out what spots gone be jumping off.

I don't go out much, but I remembered that Cleveland do its thing. And for some reason the city be lit up on Sunday nights. I can say that these people are better than me 'cause I never understood how they could kick it all night and still manage to wake up in the morning and go to work. I respect that. But I got a job of my own right now. And I take it serious. Yep. I'm the supervisor of a tree company. Illegal trees; but hey, it's a job.

So call me the decider and the provider. And if this is what I have to do to reach my goal, then so be it.

After we got done walking off them burgers and milkshakes, I headed straight to Felicia's house because she had to help her father with a restaurant business lay-out. And before she got out the car she gave me a long kiss goodbye.

"Ma, you think that we can do brunch tomorrow? How about it?"

"Most likely, Ta," she said, gazing at me like she was love struck. "I'ma call you in a few hours. You better answer yo' phone when I call. And don't be messing with them dusty hoes, B.M.s included."

"Yeah right, Ma. You know I don't get down like that. Call me in a minute, Boo, alright?"

"Alright be safe, Ta. Real safe," she said, stressing the point.

"I will, Boo. See you in a minute."

This nigga, Black, ain't called me yet. Fuck it. I've been having a good time all weekend, so I can spend this time alone for good use.

Words from my old Karate teacher…, he said, "Ta, one who stays with a crowd daily is one whose mind is crowded daily."

So I circled my street twice and made sure that nobody was pending my moves, backed up into the garage and turned off the alarm system.

I went into the house and lit up my dip stick and proceeded with doing my stretches and breathing exercises.

"'Hello." Right when I'm in the groove, the phone interrupts.

"Yeah, bohhy, what up?" said Black.

"Man, what's up?" I replied.

"Shiit, you tell me." I blew out the dip stick and picked up my keys. "Yeah, I'm 'bout to come get you, my nig. Is you done being Romeo for the day?" I said, joking around. I headed out to the car.

"Ahhh, whatever, man. I swear you was on that shit too, bohhy."

I was 'bout to comment on that when my phone beeped.

"Man, hold on." I clicked over. "Hello," I said, pulling off, going to Black's house.

"My nigga, why the fuck is you tripping?" It was Slick. "How long do you think I'm supposed to wait for you? Look we gone have to try this shit again tomorrow," he said.

"Shiit, hold up, Slick. I'm on my way right now. Matter-of fact, I'm less than ten minutes away." I turned the car around and headed to Slick's. I seriously needed to handle this shit today.

"Look, you got the keys, right?" I asked.

"Man, what kinda dumb ass question is that to ask the Landlord? Meathead." Slick said. "You still got the cash right?"

"Hell yeah, bohhy."

"I mean all of it, nigga. Everything down to the last red cent. I ain't taking no more short paper from you niggas. No more spoiling you niggas anymore," Slick said.

"Man, Slick, I want you to tell me one thing, doe. When did I start looking like them dudes from Lord of the Rings?"

"Man, you got a slick ass mouth piece," Slick said. "But I do admire your word play and game, little nigga."

"Yeah, well you know we're from the same hood," I stressed. "Eh, come outside. I'm pulling up right now."

Slick came outside and I got out the car. He dapped me up and handed me a Heiny. We discussed our leasing agreement and he filled me in on all the other stipulations of the property. "Tell them to sign this," he said, handing me the paper. "And get it back to me. You can even mail it to me if you short on yo gas money."

"Ahhh! There you go with the jokes again," I said.

"Naw, but for real, doe, Ta, this is my livelihood so I'm basically holding you responsible for this tenant."

"So, I guess that means I get twenty-five percent too, right?"

"Ahhh!" Slick said. "Naw, but what it do mean is that I'ma sue yo ass if y'all fuck up my shit."

"Man, get out of here," I replied. "I'll call you in a minute, my nig," I said, and went to get in my car.

*Call from . . .* "Hello, what's up?" I stopped in my tracks and answered the phone before it finished telling me who was calling.

"What's up? I thought you were on your way?" Black said.

"Yeah, my bad," I said. "I'm 'bout to come get you so you can check out yo new flat," I said. We ended the call. I looked over at Slick while I was opening up the car door. "Slick, I'm out. I'ma holla at you in a minute."

"Oh yeah, Ta, before you leave, let me get some of that good Loud," Slick said, and walked over to me.

"Ain't nothing shaking really," I said to Slick. "My man only got ounces, but he's not doing nothing until tomorrow 'cause I know you go to sleep early."

"Man, call me if you really trying to get some paper, Ta. Remember, I raised you, nigga."

"Alright. I'll hit you up at 12:01. And if you ain't out there then that's on you, my nig, 'cause this shit's going like shit off the dollar menu," I said.

"Yeah, I bet," Slick said and smirked. "In a minute, doe, right?"

"In a minute." We clapped heads and parted.

Man, this dude, Will, ain't called yet, I thought to myself as I drove off. I'ma have to call him because the only reason I haven't called him already is 'cause I'ma hate to have to turn this puppy over. So I headed back to get Black, then I called Will."

"Hello."

"Yeah, Will. What's up?"

"Ta, what's going on?" Will acted like he was happy to hear from me.

"Oh yeah, I meant to call you, man. I done fucked around and missed my flight and Galena done suffered from a heat stroke. So now we're in Orlando and she's in the hospital. The doctor said that she'll be alright. Our flight got rescheduled so I probably won't be home for another couple of days. I just want to make sure she's in good condition before we head home. Will went on saying, "Ta, if you get your car, then you can gone head and leave the Cutty in the driveway."

"Naw, Will, it ain't that serious, man. I'm more so worried about Galena. She gone be okay, right?" I asked.

"Yeah-yeah, man, she'll be fine and I'll pay you for keeping the car for me, too," Will said.

"Will," I shook my head. "Will, you don't never got to do that. You wanted my honest opinion on the car, and the truth is that bitch goes dumb hard," I said.

"Oh yeah?" Will said.

"I swear, Will. I mean, the engine is unexplainable," I added.

"Well, that's good to hear," Will said.

"You haven't got into any troubles have you?" asked Will.

*Only if he knew*, I thought. "Oh, hell naw, Will. You know me. I'm just as laid back as you is," I said.

"Well, I wouldn't say that, 'cause I know that you gotta little bit more energy than me. But don't worry 'bout us. Me and the wife a be home in a few days."

"That's cool and I'll keep y'all in my prayers. Call me when you touch down, OG. Peace," I said as I closed the phone.

Man, that's fucked up. Why do bad shit always happen to good people? That lady is one of the nicest people that I ever met personally. Well, let me keep this day moving, shake it off, and stay focused. He said she was cool so she's probably cool. Maybe they just need a little more time away from home.

## Chapter 16

Black called me back. "Where is you at?" When I told him where I was, he told me to "Just stay right there."

When he pulled up he was driving an all-black Jeep Wrangler with chrome wheels. It was kinda cool in a way. I guess he had dropped Saree off and kept her whip.

"Yeah Ta, this is what we in tonight."

"That's cool with me because this bitch is kinda low key," I said.

I mean, it really wasn't low key; but what I meant was that nobody would expect for us to be in it. I didn't have a problem with that. I mean, I had a few whips anyway. But something like this, if this was my only car, yeah, this would be gay.

Black wheeled an Excursion, but he let his BM roll it to ride the fam around. Low key incognito. Alright. Me and Bleed is on the same page now.

"Yeah, you got to sign this, Black."

"Sign what?"

"Sign this lease agreement, nigga. And here's yo key right here."

Black's face lit up. Grabbing the keys from me, he asked, "Did you see it yet?"

"Naw," I replied. "I mean, lightweight; I mean, not really. Man, shiit. Just open up the door and check it out yourself."

He opened the door, and I can't lie, Slick really did have that bitch looking plushed out. And on top of that, that bitch had mirrors all around the walls.

"Man, I'ma get a stripper pole in this bitch off rip," Black said, while pacing around, amped up, going from room to room.

The nigga's face had lit all the way up, I swear. I ain't never seen my nigga smile like that. Even with Saree he still had a slight guard up.

"Ta, good looking, man," he said, dapping me up and hugging at the same time.

"Man, don't thank me, thank Slick. We got to break this bitch in, doe," I said.

"You already know. Go head and tap something."

We smoked a wet square at the table and planned where we were going. Our plan was to stay out from 12am until 12pm. 'The Cotton Club, karaoke up at Tonight's Palace, alright. The Rock Bottom, alright. Peabody's local concerts. Yeah, that bitch too.' That's the extra shit, 'cause hopefully, when we turn these phones back on, this bitch jumps super hard.

And the weed man usually would be sleep by 12 o'clock. Or they'll be just scared to come out. Plus, with me holding back on them pounds, it makes it so nobody besides us gets nothing.

We was sitting eye-to-eye, intense conversation, strategizing like two coaches trying to win the big game.

"I gotta take the car back to the house if I'm riding with you," I said.

"Why don't you just leave it in my garage?" Black said, playing with the garage remote, laughing. "You know you are in the heights, so what's gonna happen to it?"

Black's swag was through the roof, feeling his new spot to the fullest.

"Ahhh!" I said. "Oh you fly now, huh? Now that's what I'm talking bout," I said, giving Black a hand clap-dap, hug style.

I grabbed the bowling ball bags out the whip and put them in the Jeep. It was about 10 o'clock, so I had a few mo' things to take care of.

We smoked a few more squares, so of course one of us was hooking up with my nigga, Murder. But before we did, I told Black to run me on Union real quick so I could put this money in my

BM's mailbox. Once we got there, I put it in an envelope and then tipped off the porch. When I got back in the car I called her.

"Ta, what the fuck do you want?" she said, without even a "hello."

"Ma, I ain't want shit. I was about to come say hi, but it looked like you had company."

"Negative," she said. I could just picture her talking with her lips twisted up. "All I do is work. Plus, I don't do company on Sundays."

"Well, it ain't nothing. I mean, I can't explain, but my letter that I left for you in the mailbox should tell you everything."

"What? Boy, I'm going out there right now to see what yo' crazy butt is talking about." I waited while she checked. "Ta, it ain't no letter in here; just an envelope with about. . ." She paused for a second. She seemed slightly in shock. "Well, you know how much it is. Of course you do. Okay thanks, Boo," Erica said.

"Boo. Ahhhh! I see how it is now," I said. "Naw, but I'll do anything for the mother of my daughter."

"Yeah, she asked about you, too."

"Well, tell her that daddy will come see her tomorrow. Sweet dreams."

We headed back out and got back to business. First stop, my nigga Murder, though, to get us some water.

I whipped off four hundred dollars and he said, "Man, I ain't even know who y'all was. My nigga, y'all was about to get painted," Murder said.

"Murder, I guess when they made your .40 caliber, you must have been the only nigga to get one," I said.

"Man, what is you trying to say?" Murder asked.

Both me and Black upped our hammers. "We saying we keep ours on us, too. Cocked and ready," I said. We both laughed.

Murder was looking shocked at first-then his facial expression changed to more of a proud look from knowing that his niggas stay strapped.

"Man, let me get that four hundred," Murder said, smiling.

I always fucks with Murder. He was a cool breed of a nigga. You know a lot of dealers tends to soften up after they touched a certain amount of cash. But this nigga stayed solid. Plus, he never tried to play us like smokers. Some niggas understood that we got high mainly for recreation.

"Look, I got two kinds. I got that light clear mellow__and I got that dark yellow gorilla piss. So which one do y'all want?"

"Look, Murder, let us get both. Half-light and a half of that gorilla."

"Bet," Murder said and handed us two bottles.

"Damn, Murder. I hope that's a grill." I was being sarcastic talking about his gold teeth.

"Ta, don't worry about what it is, 'cause you ain't put shit on this mouthpiece, nigga," he said.

"Ahhh!" Me and Black said at the same time. That was the expression we used when somebody said some fly shit. We hit them off with "Ahhh!"

"Ta, I heard you got a new Cutty. And I heard that the bitch is mean, too."

"Well, you know," I said. "That shit's a small thing to a giant."

Eh, what can I say? A nigga's never too big to cap a little, right? Besides, when I make enough skrilla I plan on buying that bitch from Will anyway. *Hell yeah, I'ma buy it*, I thought to myself. Have everybody speaking Japanese like, YUJUSCOP? 'Yes, I just copped, suckas.'

Ahhhh! Midnight hit and it was on. Sitting outside the Cotton Club, my phone got to hopping off rip. "*Call from__*

"Yeah, hello," I answered.

"Yeah, what's up? This Peaches."

"Oh yeah. What's up, Ma?"

"Can you come meet me at the Cotton Club. Yeah. Alright, then call me when you get up here."

"Yeah, hello. Who? Treasure and Tam? Black you know them?" I asked, looking over at Black.

"Yeah, the twins. They cool peoples," Black said.

"Oh, Peaches gave y'all the number. Alright, well meet me in the lot at the Cotton Club."

"Fat Luth, what's up?"

"Ta, what's good, man? Tell me everything's back together."

I sighed and said, "nope, shit still fucked up, Luth. But I got__

Luth cut me off. "I know," he said. "All you got is ounces. Man, where is yo tight ass at anyway?"

"I'm at the Cotton Club."

"Man, Ta, when did you start clubbing?"

"Man, I said 'I'm up here.' I ain't say I was clubbing."

"Alright then. I should be up there in 5.5."

"What, minutes?" I asked.

"Naw, seconds nigga," Luth said, banging on the windows, scaring the shit out of me and Black.

"Man, Luth! Why is yo fat ass always playing," I said. I had to regroup. He had really scared me.

"How the fuck did you know we was in the Jeep anyway?"

"Nigga, this is my spot. This is where I grind and put my mac hand down on the little brizzles. Plus, girly over there I was trying to holla at with the blondish-reddish hair told me y'all had it over here."

"Peaches?" I asked.

"Yeah, that's her. When she said yo name, I told her, I know that lame."

"Ahhhh! Lame, huh? Man, what is you trying to do?" I asked putting my hustling face back on.

"Man, I got five hundred," Luth said, while trying to peel money off the top of his knot. "Man, Ta, take this or leave it. If you don't, I ain't fucking with you no mo."

"Man, Luth, you killing me. Man, give me $550 and we're cool."

"Damn, nigga, that's cutting into my drinking money. Ta, you sure is a hard bargain."

"Luth, that's a deal, man. Everybody gots to pay six hundred and I'm charging you five hundred-fifty."

"Yeah, whatever. I still got love for you, my nigga, but you need to get them pounds back rolling," said Luth. "Is y'all coming in?"

"Naw, man, we about to slide to Melodies, then the Rock Bottom."

"Man, what the fuck is y'all on?" Luth said.

"Pirating," I said at the same time Black said it. We clapped each other's hands.

"Eh, Luth, real talk, doe. I'ma fuck with you real tough. Just sit tight and roll with these punches for a minute. Now go trick off yo weed and get some booty," I said, laughing with Black on some light weight two-faced type shit, but just playing, doe.

My phone rang "Eh where's you at?" It was Slick. "I'm here. I don't see you."

"Pull in the lot and you'll see me," I said.

"Man, where in the fuck is you at?" This time he said it like he was in a hurry. "Ta, I don't see yo truck."

"That's 'cause I'm not in my truck. Pull in the damn lot, man."

"Man, you got me in this hot ass lot. Bohhy, you tripping." Slick pulled up in a new truck, late as usual.

I walked over to the truck and Slick waved his hand, meaning get in the back. I jumped in the back seat like, "Damn, you got this bitch lit up."

"Yeah," he said. "A little deal on some screens. I had to jump on. It ain't nothing, doe."

Slick had a cold ass model looking bitch in the front with him.

"Eh, what's up, babe?" I said.

"This is Michelle, Ta. But matter-of-fact it's Ms. Michelle to you, 'cause you still a little young ass boy."

Slick sat in the front seat talking, making his girl blush. I could tell she was feeling his swag and his smart remarks.

*'Man, this nigga always got some ole Superfly shit to say,'* I thought to myself, but I never come short, doe.

"How much, my nig?"

"Six hundred an ounce," I said

"Man, you killing 'em out here." He shook his head. "Shiit man, you killing me. Damn, man, fuck it. Give me four of them. Twenty-four, right? Man, I'm going on strike after this. Y'all out here trying to break a nigga. Between yo prices and her just throwing shit in the bag, I'ma have to sling nickel bags just to make it out this bitch," Slick said, shaking his head as if he was taking a beating; acting like his money was funny, which was a hustle tactic that I had picked up from him."

"Alright, man. Who's in the Jeep with you?"

"Oh, that's Black."

"Black? Oh tell my nigga I said, what's up," Slick said, unlocking the automatic lock doors, letting me out.

I went and jumped back in the whip with Black, and Slick pulled up on the side of us bumping some old M.C. Eight from the *Menace to Society* soundtrack.

"Eh, hit the window, Black."

Black rolled down the window. "What's up, bohhhy!" he said to Slick.

"I can't call it. Just sucking up some of this good oxygen," Slick replied.

"Eh, 'good looking' on the spot."

"Yeah, you already know you're good for it all day long, my nigga. Just stay low and keep the traffic down, ya heard? Unless it's shit like this going in and out that bitch," Slick said, pointing to Michelle. "But it probably won't be 'cause this is some grown man type shit and y'all still some little ass boys," he said, and skirted off into traffic.

*Skuuuuurrr!*

"Damn, did you detect a little haterism?" I asked Black, smiling.

"Yeah, I felt that, but it's a good thing that I had my hater guard up," Black said, laughing.

See, Slick was our real nigga, and we knew that he was just playing, but for real I could sense some hate coming from somewhere. I just couldn't pinpoint exactly where it was coming from.

"Eh, doe, you know what I say? Fuck 'em. Yeah. Hell yeah, fuck 'em all."

The phone rang. I grabbed it up and answered the call. "Yeah, I'ma bout to be right there," I said, because I knew who it was but they didn't say anything. "Hello?" I smiled when they finally said something. "Damn, Bleed, you already up there? Alright, I ain't never been up there but I'm headed to you now. Here talk to the driver."

"Hello," Black said. "You and yo girl is trying to do what?" Black looked over at me, smiling.

I shook my head, "No," straight pirating.

"Yeah, I'm with that later," Black said. "But right now we was trying to do something on the tree side. Alright, we'll be right there."

Man, a niggas phone was cranking, you hear me? Jumping out the park, on a Sunday night, too.

We hit every club, bar spot and after hour joints there was. Plus, all the word-of mouth sites, too.

A nigga had to fill up twice, and I ain't talking 'bout gas either.

We pulled up at Auntie's house about five in the morning. Auntie sent me her usual and a few more of her friends who was either trying to smoke before they went on their temp jobs, or was trying to extend their powder or crack highs. But the best clientele she plugged me in with was all the dope boys from her hood. Them niggas would be like, 'y'all niggas is taxing a lot for that shit.' But fuck it, 'cause we were the only ones out.

We stayed around Auntie's house until 10am. Shiiit we even posted up at all the blood banks and plasma centers early. I hate for them people to have to spend their donation money on weed. But shiit, who am I fooling? They was going to spend it on trees anyway. At least people know that they're getting good weed from me. And this is what I'll do since I'm a nice guy and I don't want to see you pass out. I'll leave them five dollars so they can get something to eat. And if they spend it on cigarettes then that's on them, buddy.

"Black, let's be out."

We shot to his house so we could count the money. I knew we had $14,200 from Saturday night. I counted the day's take.

"I got $8,400 right here," I said out loud. How much did you count on?"

"$10,600."

"Man, you telling me that we made $19,000 on a Sunday night? That's almost twenty geez."

That shit woke me straight up. "This shit is crazy," I said.

# Chapter 17

"Hello, Ta. What's up?"

"Shiit me. Sometimes you," I said. "What's up, Boo?" Felicia's call had woke me up.

"What's happening, is this certain Prince that I know was supposed to take me out to brunch this afternoon," Felicia said.

"Oh yeah, I thought I was supposed to take you."

"Ta, quit playing," she said, laughing.

"Alright. I had to work late so I'm 'bout to come and get you now; well, as soon as I get dressed," I added, reaching my left arm down to the floor, feeling around for my boots.

"Yeah, 'cause I was looking at my iPod and it's a very nice Italian place that I want to go to. They have a special on some new giant ravioli filled with mozzarella cheese and mushrooms. And the best thing about them is that they're made from scratch."

"Yeah, I'm with that. Just give me a few minutes. I gots to slide to my spot." I stood up and stretched. "I fell asleep over Black's new spot. I'ma get dressed and be right there."

"Ta, can you hurry up 'cause I'm hungry," she whined in her spoiled daddy's girl voice.

"Alright then let me go, Ma," I said, rushing her off the phone so I could move faster.

"See you in a minute, Boo. Smooches," she said, before hanging up.

I shoulda still been sleep, but when the paper starts to roll in, a nigga be up like the sun. Believe that. Now when I'm out here, it feels like I got something to live for. Another call. "Hello," I said. Black's voice came through the phone. "What up, sleepy head?"

"My dude. Why is you playing, calling me from the other room?" I know I sounded cranky but I was still tired.

"Man, the other room? Hah! My dude, I been gone. I had to drop off my little breezy to her exercise class."

"You on your way back?"

"In a minute. I'm at a drive thru window trying to buy a pack of Newport's. What time is you trying to link up?"

"After I handle this business. So, I'll say in about three hours. We're starting early today, right?"

"Yeah that's cool," he replied.

"Eh, how in the fuck do I 'pose to lock the door?"

"Man, just turn the knob. Ain't shit in that bitch to steal anyway. What a couch, refrigerator, and coffee table?" Black said.

"Alright, bet. Then I'll see you in a minute, bet?"

"Bet."

I went to the house and jumped in some Italian gear; some clothing for the occasion. Before I went to pick up Felicia, I put the old school in the garage and pulled out the truck.

It was a couple of weeks before summer started. The weather was about seventy-five degrees. When I went to pick up Felicia, she came out with a thin Valentino trench coat that came down to her knees, but it had a split that went all the way up her thigh. I can't lie, this chick was a diamond. We went on 90 toward the west side. When we pulled into Lakewood she told me to pull up in this little mini-park area, a few streets from the restaurant.

"Man, Felicia, what is we turning in here for?"

"Ta, I gotta show you something. Pull right under this tree," she said.

I backed in under the tree and I'm thinking that she's 'bout to show me some sentimental stuff, but she started licking her lips in a real seductive way, and smiling.

"Ta, don't you want your dessert before you eat your main course," she said, pulling her coat up.

I can't explain what she had on under that coat. Let's just say, 'nothing at all.'

Man, this was the best girl that I ever had. Yeah, my girl's a straight freak and it don't get no better than this. She said 'if that was good then we can do round two after dinner.' Man, lil' Ma got a nigga dizzy. You feel me?

"Hello, Madame, may I please take your order," the waitress addressed her.

"Yeah, I would like to try the ravioli with Italian sausage. And I'll take a salad also."

"Yeah, and I'll take the ravioli, plus the veal parmesan. And let me get a salad, too. And some of your top shelf red wine."

For the demo that Felicia put down; I shoulda bought her a case of that shit.

"Ta, what's wrong? Why you keep looking at the phone," Felicia asked.

"Cause, Bay, I got a few moves to make in a minute."

Only if she knew that I wanted this shit to be over with, meaning the grind; over, just so I could be with her for the rest of my life.

I still had my guard up, 'cause nigga, this is Cleveland and females is hard on a nigga here. I wasn't no slouch, but I done had my share of fucked up relationships too.

Like the time when I did my first number in jail for eighteen months. I was twenty and my girlfriend, Angel, told me to come to her house when I got released. But when I arrived she was standing in the doorway with her hair sweated out.

"Hey, Sweety," she said. "I meant to tell you that things kinda changed a little bit."

Some old nigga came out from the back in his boxer shorts and was like, "Yeah this is me now, little nigga." And to make it so bad, I had just been locked up with the nigga. I had him make a three-way call for me. He kept her number and knocked her off.

Man, I busted every window that I seen. I flipped out! And the police ended up getting to me before I could get to my pistol.

That was a blessing for me, 'cause even though I went back to jail that night for disturbing the peace and vandalism, I was on my way to catching a body. And you know the pen is full of niggas that's doing life over a hoe.

Or what about when I was twenty-four and I had lost my job and my hustle hand was dead. I was messing with this stallion named Kim. Before I fell off, it was, "Oooh, Daddy, I love you. Give me a kiss, and can you please fuck me, Daddy, 'cause you're so sexy." Right?

But after I fell off, it was, "Nigga, you gonna have to get yo broke, lame, non-hustling, bum ass off of my couch, 'cause, I'm really about to have company." Just like that. No warning or nothing. Man, I sure do get the hard ones for real.

Then it was Trisha. I fucked with her up until shit kept coming up missing. Yeah, I found out that girly had sneaky habits. My nephews even clowned me for that one.

"Damn, Unc! How you ain't know that girly was a crack head? You slipping for that one," one of them said.

Naw, I didn't know until the PS3, weed and digital scale came up missing out the blue.

Then you got the drama of all drama…my baby's mother, Erica. I squared up with her brothers various times for some of the dumbest shit. Her attitude was past through. It was thaaroooooooo!

"Ta, who smoked my last black and mild?" Erica asked.

"I did, Boo. I'm 'bout to go get some more in a minute," I had told her.

Erica flared up. "In a minute? Uh-un! You 'bout to go get them now, bitch ass nigga."

"Huh?"

"You heard me, nigga. I don't care what you do on the streets, but you ain't gone bully me," she said, with an aggressive tone, pushing her finger into my forehead.

"Ma, it was only a mild," I said, grabbing her wrist and moving her hand away from my face.

"Fuck that!" She screamed and went stomping into her bedroom and shut the door. Then she started yelling, "I'm 'bout to call my brothers to come fuck you up."

Yeah, just like that. Them niggas tried to jump me so many times that I just got tired of it and let one of them niggas have it.

*Thadow! Thadow!* "Bitch, back up!" Then they tried to press charges, but I knew how to get low. And when I did end up getting jammed, you know what they say – no gun, no case.

*"Sorry Your Honor, but my baby's mother suffers from a severe case of tri-polar. And as far as this man being shot, I have no clue on who would do such a thing. They all need mental help if you ask me."*

"Ta! Ta! Is you gone answer your phone," Felicia said, rousing me from my daydream.

"Hello? Yeah, what up, Black? I'll meet up with you in about an hour." I hung up and motioned for our server. "Waiter, check please."

"Yeah, round two gone have to jump off tonight," I told Felicia. "I got business to take care of right now." On the way to Felicia's house I didn't say much.

"Ta, is something wrong?" she asked.

"Naw, Bay," I replied while I ran my hand gently through her hair, then over her ear. "I just gotta work, and I can't be late."

I pulled up and gave her a kiss, and when she was getting out I said, "Ma that was the best dessert that I had ever in my twenty-seven years of living."

She pulled me by my shirt and kissed me again, and said, "Ta you is caraaazzzy. Call me in a minute. Smooches."

# Chapter 18

*Day three on the grind.*

I'm lovin' this shit. Every minute of it. Especially if today is going to be anything like the weekend.

Black told me to park, and that he'd be there to get me again. I guess him and Saree got some type of understanding 'cause their system been working out real smooth.'

This hand-to-hand grind was different. More of a shrewd grind, but I liked it, doe, 'cause I felt the hustle and the muscle. Plus I stayed sharp from working and all the movement which had my mind constantly moving.

I swear, I told so many lies that I started believing that shit myself. *"Ta, you got back, right?"*

*"Shiit, I just ran out of PS. I got these zones, doe;"* or *"My connect just got knocked so you gone have to holla at my man. Yeah, hello. Yeah, I'm still waiting but I can do a little something."* My favorite one is, *"Man, I don't really get down no more. Yeah, I quit hustling, but shiiit, since you always been my peeps, then I can sell you something out of my personal stash."*

I heard that in the end of your life you're accounted for all the lies you told. Well, I hope the Lord see that it was for a good reason, but if not, I know I'm going down.

Peaches hooked us up with her friend, Ronisa, and she didn't mind if we posted up around her crib as long as we shoot her a few dollars, plus some good tree. She was a little older than us, so all she asked us to be was discreet. I didn't believe in stretching shit out, you know, having niggas sitting around, playing shit off. Look, I'm on a mission. I'm grinding hard, and Black back there with you in his scope. So bullshit if you want, 'cause he is trained and ready to go for whenever funny shit pops off.

My phone rang. "Hello."

"Yeah, I need my usual." It was Lil' Man.

"Yeah, I ain't got nothing like you usually do."

I wasn't trying to get myself caught up like last time when he had me pull in the back and be surrounded by his goons. "Plus," I said, "I'm across the way and can't really move right now."

"Man, Ta, I just need to get my hands on a little something to hold me over. Yeah, and I'm driving too. So can I meet you?" Lil' Man asked.

"Oh yeah? You got wheels, huh? Well, meet me on the Dale off 116th Street," I said.

"Bet," Lil' Man replied.

"Bet. Call me when you get on the street," I told Lil' Man, before hanging up the phone.

We posted on the Dale for like two hours. Then Ronisa plugged us with her girl, Lisa. She said that we could come through there long as we give her a few dollars too. Shiit, I realized that everybody wanted to be a part of something. This was our Westside spot. We'd post up here for a few more hours, shoot to Auntie's house at the end of the night, and end the night there.

I looked in the phone and called Lil' Man back. He still hadn't showed up or called. His phone went straight to voicemail. Twice. It had been more than two hours since he had called. "Fuck it." I was out to the west side to set up shop and tonight we'd shoot our regular over at Auntie's house.

I was selling anywhere from ten dollar sticks to one gram for twenty dollars. Quarters after quarters, half ounces and ounces. That shit was going, bohhy. I was heating up. Feel me?

"Put something in the air," I said, sounding like I was fired up from all the movement.

"Tap something then, nigga," Black said, seeming like he was feeding into my energy too.

"You ain't said nothing but a word, nigga. Tap something," I said, amped up.

"We been smoking that mellow for the last few days, so let's see what this gorilla do," Black said.

"Bet," I said. "Cause we smoke all day anyway, so it can't be all like that, right?" I said, sounding unsure if he wanted to smoke, thinking that it might be too potent. He put the cigarette in the bottle. He didn't even have to pull on it. He turned the square upside down and it just ran down the cigarette.

"Yeah, that's oils right there," we both agreed.

He lit the square and he pretty much knew by the texture that it was dear mamma. I took a pull like it wasn't gorilla and all of a sudden everything got to slowing down. My mouth tightened up and my eyebrows went down like I was mean mugging the world. For about two minutes I felt myself zooming through a tunnel of lights, then it felt like my fucking molecules had split apart then came back together at the same time. My focus started coming back, then I looked over at Black and it looked like he was going through the same thing. "Is you alright?" I said.

"Shit, I am now. I was high as fuck fo' a minute, doe," Black said, shaking his head like he was shaking off a high.

Man, I'm telling you, doe, it wasn't nothing laid back about this shit, for real. It was one plus to it, doe. It intensified the grind.

"Ten dollar sticks? Naw, it ain't no more ten dollar nothing, my nig. You gots to have twenty or better." Another customer was up.

"Man, I'm out of shit for twenty. You gone have to grab an eighth. Take it or leave it."

That's what I told them and they would take it, 'cause really the gleam in our eyes meant business, and they knew it.

"Hello."

"Yeah, Ta. I'm on the Honeydale right now." Finally Lil' Man called back.

"Damn, my nigga. I'm on the Westside now. I tried to call yo line a few times and kept getting a voicemail. I even waited for another hour and some change. You can come over this way, doe," I said.

"Come over that way? Man, what the fuck you think, that I'm trying to be on a wild goose chase?" Lil Man sounded angry in the phone. "You said call when I got on the Dale, nigga. Fuck you having me come up here for nothing, nigga?"

"Look, my nigga. I ain't in the business of waiting. My nigga, you can meet me over here or chalk it," I said, with veins popping out of my forehead. Lil' Man started talking to somebody in the background.

"This hoe ass nigga on the line talking real foxy" he said.

"I waited for you for almost two hours," I said. "You ain't show up, nigga. So, I kept it pushing."

"Man, who the fuck is that?" Black asked.

"This lil' lame from yo neck of the woods."

"Man, hand me that phone," Black said. I put it on speaker and handed it over.

"Hello. What's up? I mean like what's the fucking problem, lil boy?" Black was mad.

"Lil boy? Man, Black, you know niggas is getting paid for that shit now, right?" Lil' Man said.

"Gettin' paid for what?" Black asked.

"Getting paid for being a fuck boy," Lil Man said, busting out laughing with his homies in the background.

"Ahhh! Naw, see I could never be that. But what I can be is a funeral planner, nigga. You already know me. What? What?" echoed loud from Black being heated from the remark that Lil' Man made.

"Man, I'm in the bricks all day, every day, Black. So what's up?"

"Yep, and I'll be there to holla at you; Lil bitch ass nigga," Black said, looking salty. Lil Man had pissed him off to the fullest.

"Come on, Ta. We bout to go holla at this nigga," he said, with his teeth clinched. He pushed the phone into me and gripped his hammer.

"Hell naw, we ain't going down there," I said. "That nigga got a way of getting to you. Fuck that nigga, Black. We're 'bout to get this money."

"That nigga called me a fuck boy," Black said, with the salty face, shaking his head. "You heard him."

"You right. You my nigga so he ain't never 'bout to get that one off. Yeah, we 'bout to go down there."

"Shiit, let's roll then." Black's frown turned into a smile from knowing that his ace got his back fully.

Me and this nigga was sliding to the Bricks two deep. Yeah, just us. And you know that these niggas is usually twenty deep, but fuck it, 'cause this my nigga, doe. And if this shit gone go down, then it's going down then.

We pulled up crazy like we were the vice or something. Them niggas was only about eight deep, luckily for us. They started scattering like we was working with choppas. We jumped out the whip as soon as we seen Lil Man. He was stuck, like he ain't really think that we was gonna blow down on him.

Black jumped out and off rip, he said, "Nigga, what's up with that shit you was hollering 'bout on the line?"

"Lil Man said, "You heard me, nigga. I ain't stuttin a nigga. Niggas is getting paid to be__" and right before he was about to say it – *"Whaam!"* Black smacked him across the face with the .40. Then we started buzzing at the remaining niggas around. Shiit, I knew that it was instant beef now. Shiit, that nigga was knocked out, so I hit his pockets and got six racks off him. His boys would have hit him for it anyway.

After I hit dude's pockets, we jumped back in the Jeep and bailed. I did leave an ounce in his pocket, doe. Shiit, I figured at least he got what he asked for.

We pulled out the lot crazy, the same way that we drove in. Some of his niggas started letting off shots, just missing the jeep. We rolled a few streets up.

"Eh, turn up in here," I said, pointing to a little safe spot, "for now."

# Chapter 19

I counted off three stacks and handed them to Black, then I let him know that from now on, if it ain't about no paper, then I ain't on it. He said, 'Bet.' Then we dapped on that.

I got a call from a chick named Pandora. Her number didn't look familiar, but she told me what kinda wheels I got. She said that she met me before in a Porsche truck and that she met me at the Cotton Club.

"Oh yeah, I remember," I said.

But I was breaking rules from being too geeked up, 'cause I didn't remember her. I just didn't care at the time.

"Yo, I'm down on 80th and Woodland. Meet me at the station," I said.

I pulled up in the station and called her but the phone went straight to voicemail. I thought nothing of it then. The whole situation left my mind when I seen this nigga, Rino, in a brand new Camaro, capping as usual.

My mind had shifted soon as I seen the nigga; still thinking about the theatrics that he pulled last week, telling everybody that he made me tuck my chain. Straight up hoe shit. Damn, I really ain't want to see this nigga up here driving his bitch car and flexing. I really was ready to pop this nigga off.

Fuck it. We got to make sure it ain't no bullet holes in the Jeep. Then just like I thought, here this dumb nigga come. Since we had just bust that move in the Bricks, the plan was to be cool right now and get the fuck back to the Westside.

I was thinking that I should just do this nigga, but I gots to practice what I preach to my little nigga, Black.

"What up, Ta? I see y'all brought the Tracker out," Rino said, giggling. "Damn! Them bitches still on the market? That is a Tracker, right?" Rino said.

"Naw, my nigga. It's a Jeep. What's up, doe?" I said. I was feeling, and I'm sure, looking, aggravated from Rino's presence.

"Ain't shit really up; you know, just balling on these bitches," he said. "Oh yeah, what's up with you and Felicia?"

"Huh?" I frowned up. "What the fuck you mean?" I said.

"Man, calm down. I don't mess with her or nothing like that. No more." He added the last part under his breath on the sneak side.

"What?" I said.

"I just heard that y'all was at the set together. That's all. And I thought it was funny," Rino said. Then Rino went on saying, "cause I thought that she was a little bit out of your league, right?"

"Out of my league?" I said, sounding tremendously offended. I bit my lip and reached for my waist. This nigga is right in front of me talking reckless.

"Yeah, Ta, let me get one of those little sacks that you be having, so a nigga can get his head right," Rino said.

"Lil sacks, huh?" I said.

Then out the blue a thought came to my head.

"Yeah, you want a ten dollar stick of weed, right? I'ma make that up for you right now."

I told Black to pull on the side of the street. I wanted to be out of the camera view of the gas station. I ran over and hopped halfway in the car, then told Black to hurry up and put some of that gorilla on this weed.

"Man, you trying to smoke some wet weed?" Black asked.

"Naw. Man, hurry up. It ain't for me."

He poured a nice amount on the Loud and put it in a dime bag.

"I'll be right back." I went and jumped on the passenger's side of Rino's car.

I had a feeling that somebody was watching me. Out the side of my eye it seemed like somebody had pulled up and watched me jump into Rino's car. I didn't know for sure but I thought that it was whoever it was that had that girl call me. Fuck it. My mind was stuck on this disrespectful ass nigga right now.

Looking around, I made sure that I didn't see no peoples watching. I knew nobody had seen me when I had got in the jeep with Black.

"Yeah, I fatted it up for you my nigga," I said, smiling. "But you can just give me ten."

"Alright, but my nigga's cross sacks be a little chunky," Rino said.

"Oh don't worry about it, doe, my Nig, 'cause that shit gone have you high. High as fuck, ya heard me?" I said with a grin on my face.

"Man, I got to go grab a Swisher," Rino said.

"Yeah, just grab me a pack of cigarettes," I said, and handed him a ten dollar bill.

Rino came back with the squares and gave me three dollars in change.

"Eh, slide me around there where I'm parked at," I said.

We pulled around the corner and the Jeep was in the cut. I got out of Rino's car and hopped in the Jeep.

I know that shit was dirty, selling Rino that laced weed, but fuck it, 'cause it was less dirty than what I was going to do to him. That nigga's a hater anyway.

"Where we to?" Black said.

"Shiit we back to the Westside, I guess."

But for some reason I didn't feel like sitting back. I was still amped up and heating up.

"Man, I'm thinking 'bout hopping in the whip and hitting that freeway before it gets too late," I said. "I'm trying to double or triple these dollars that we just came up on," I said.

"What? You talking about hitting a dice game?" Black asked.

"Yeah, but in Detroit, doe."

"Ahhh! You trying to hit the casino," Black said.

"Yes sir," I said, counting the money we just got from Lil' Man. I smacked his leg with the pile of money. "I told you my hand still feels hot, my nigga."

"Shiit, alright. I'm with that too," Black said.

"I was gone pick up Felicia to slide with me, and be out," I said, testing Black, trying to see if he really was trying to roll. Black bent a couple of corners, then he looked over at me.

"Shiit, I got the Jeep until whenever. Saree ain't gotta be nowhere tomorrow. "But shiit, it's going to take them about another hour and forty-five minutes, and time is money. Plus, we still supposed to be grinding tonight. I can drop that tree off right now, then jump right on the freeway and we can still make it back and make that third shift over Auntie's house tonight," Black said.

"Shiit, you know what? You're right," I said. "Tap something out the mellow bottle, doe. We out."

I dropped off everything but a quarter pound. I knew that Black wanted to roll, but I played it off. I didn't want to seem like everything was my idea, you know. Let the young'un call a few shots too. We straight to the casino, doe; Blackjack or the crap table.

Fuck it. I'm on that Blackjack shit tonight and Black chose shooting dice.

# Chapter 20

"Player, you got sixteen. Hit or stay?"

"Shiit, hit me," I said.

When the dealer flipped that card, it was a five. I knew it. My hand felt hot. Forty-five minutes later, I turned three thousand dollars into twenty thousand. I lost three straight hands and ended up leaving with eighteen thousand. Shiit. I knew when to get off that table this time.

I looked over at Black and he was talking big shit at the table. The combination of water and alcohol had him on that level.

"Nigga, I'm from the Bricks. This is what we do all day, every day. Watch 'point.'" He made about $15,000 racks, and since he had two fans standing close to him, he got to talking mo' shit.

"Yeah, this point right here," Black said.

"Alright, I'ma hit this one for my nigga that just walked up," Black said, referring to me.

I watched that nigga hit for $42,000 on the dice and that was unusual. I thought my hand was hot, but I swear, this nigga was on fire! He gave these two Jamaican chicks standing beside him some chips and told them to get a few drinks and keep the change. This nigga had the look of a killer in his eyes.

The phone rang. He answered. "Hello. What's up, Baby? I'm killing them right now, you hear me?" He turned and looked at me and winked his eye. "Just be ready to go shopping tomorrow, you hear me?" Black said, while he was shaking the dice. "Alright, I love you, too." He pushed the end button on the phone.

The two girls came back with the drinks, and we downed them rounds. He crapped out a few times and I'm like, "Blizzy, let's be out."

I didn't know if he was still hot but I've done witnessed losing everything in a matter of seconds. He left the table still chopping game.

"Nigga, I'm from the Brick. We ain't play with Tonka Trucks. We played with these here ivories."

He gave the Jamaican girls a kiss on the cheek and a hug, then pointed to me, and they came and did the same thing to me. I loved their hospitality. They followed us to the lot where we was parked at, then asked us if we knew where they could get some weed at.

"Shiit, right here," I said. Then the one girl, I found out her name was Sophia; she said, "I only smoke Loud. That's either Kush, Dro, or Haze."

"Well, you're in luck, Ma, 'cause I got ounces for…Uuhmm__"

Fat Luth would have wanted to kill me but they caught me at the right time. "Five hundred," I said.

"Okay," she said, with that Jamaican accent. "Give me three of them." She handed me fifteen hundred dollars. Then she handed me her number on the receipt from the drinks. That left me in a zone. Shiit, I had to show them a little love. I had come up.

On the way back, Black was like, "Man, good looking. I'm glad that you had me out there, Ta. You was killing 'em on the table, right?" Black said.

"Yes sir, this is what I do," I said, banding up my winnings, making my money look neat and crispy.

"Oh yeah, I seen how much you had my back earlier," I said.

"I respect that. And if it wasn't for you, I wouldn't have come up on this," Black said. "That's why I want you to take this." He threw ten bands on my lap.

"Naw, my nigga. You ain't gotta pay me for having yo back, my nigga," I said, with a serious look on my face.

"My nigga, if you don't take it then I'ma feel disrespected," Black said.

"Shiit. I can't believe this. Ain't nobody ever shot me something like this."

"Yeah, my nigga, I'm straight. My BMs and kids is cool and Saree is straight too; plus, you always looking out for me, Ta. So I wanna give something back," Black said.

"Man, what do you want me to do with this?" I said.

Black replied, "Nigga, do whatever with it. I don't care. Throw the shit out the window. Nigga just take it before I change my mind."

"Alright, my nigga, that's what I'm gone do. Good looking." I nodded my head. "Well, let's drop this paper off now nigga, 'cause I know we smell like money my, nigga, right?" I said.

"Eh, after we leave the house you know we gotta pass the Roc, right?" Black said. "Yeah, it's right before we get to Auntie's house," he added.

"Right. I see, you trying to go trick out a little bit, huh?" I said, grinning, rubbing my hands together."

"Naw, a nigga just had a good night, and a nigga just trying to share the wealth a little and trick out a little too. Fuck it," Black said, laughing.

"But really, I'm thinking about buying a ring for Saree, 'cause see I'm tired of playing out here," Black said with a sincere look on his face.

"Yeah? You and Saree getting married?" I said in a surprised tone.

"Yeah, who else?" Black said.

"Shiit, calm down, nigga; 'cause if you like it, I love it. Shiit. Let me tap something for the future groom. I know I can be the best man, right?"

He pulled on a cigarette and blew out smoke. "Come on man, you already know. But I think that you think that a nigga playing 'bout this shit," Black said. He ashed his square.

"Naw, 'cause I might be on the same type of shit, my Nig. In a few days we should reach our goals, then we can sit back with our girls and take trips, run some businesses, and have some more shorties. You feel me?" I said.

"A double wedding!" Black said. "Aahhh, I'm with that," he added.

"Eh, I bet that nigga, Rino taking a beating right now. Especially if he blew that blunt," I said, smirking.

"Hell yeah," Black agreed."

## Chapter 21

About the time that we was at the casino, this nigga, Rino, managed to get found butt naked, shot up, stripped, and murdered, with a half a blunt still in the ashtray. Somebody said that he was last seen talking to some dudes in a black Jeep, so guess who fit the description? This nigga had the strap on him but I still wonder who would really want to kill this nigga. He did have a reckless mouthpiece, but for real, this nigga was just a playboy type nigga, getting over on school chicks and bitches with low self-esteem; jumping in and out the game, but nowhere near major, and the nigga wasn't going to fight, shoot or even rob shit. So with all that, the shit was kinda puzzling to me.

They said Rino pulled up in his girl's driveway after he smoked that wet weed and started flipping. He just kept saying that he felt dirty so he started taking his clothes off. His girl wouldn't let him in the house because she said that he was tripping.

I heard that Rino was on the phone high as fuck, crying. They said his girl told the nigga to leave his car because she thought that he was too drunk to drive. This nigga was so high that he couldn't even talk right.

Then they said he was slurring his words. But his girl told everybody that he said, "If you ain't fucking with me, Ma, then I'ma kill myself."

So he went and jumped back in the car with no clothes on and backed out the driveway. Then when he was about to pull out he seen the jack boys in the car parked in front of the house. He rolled the window down and said, "Oh, my bad, my dude. I was looking for somebody else." I'm guessing he was looking for me. Then they said Rino started flipping.

"Nigga, you came to see my girl, didn't you?" he yelled at them. He upped his hammer on dude, but didn't shoot. Instead tears started coming out of his eyes. High as fuck, he was screaming, "nigga, I'ma kill you. Then they say dude just let off a whole clip on Rino and hit up the whole side of the car. He caught three shots in his head, lined from chest, neck to his dome.

"Hello. Yeah Boo, my bad. I know we was post to link up but something jumped off," I said.

"So what happened, Ta? Oh, let me guess. You and Black had to work late?" Felicia said.

"Yeah, pretty much so," I said. We had made it back from Detroit but was headed to the strip club.

"Ta, I'm starting not to like this."

"Ma," I said, cutting her off, "This shit will be over before you know it, and I got a surprise for you later," I said.

"A surprise, huh? Yeah, that's cool but I really just wanted to see you in the physical 'cause I miss you already, Ta."

"You do?"

"Yeah," Felicia said.

"Matter-a-fact, I got a few more drops to make then the night is over, and I'ma turn it in early. So look, Boo, I gots to go. I'll see you in a minute," I said, leaning back on the passenger's side counting my money. "Smooches," I tried to whisper.

"Smooches. Ahh! This nigga said, 'Smooches.' This nigga's checking in and talking about I'm whipped," Black said, laughing hard. He smacked the steering wheel with his hand.

"Man, whatever," I said. I switched the subject. "Why the fuck you all in my shit anyway? Come on. Let's blow some of this good paper."

We dropped the guns and the cash off and kept three racks, plus a quarter pound, 'cause shiiit, if I don't make it rain tonight at least I'll find some new custy's on the weed side.

I came off in the spot with that QP off in my draws. Lap dances was ten dollars. I gave this black, mixed with Indian looking chick twenty dollars for a dance. When she was giving me my dance I popped the question on her.

"Ma, who do you know trying to get some of this exclusive weed that I got?"

"I do, but I need to try it first because everybody that comes in here claims that they got exclusive weed, or good weed, or Dro, but most of the time it just be some Reggie Miller," said the stripper as she was grinding on my lap with her arms around my neck. She was grooving to '*I Can Read Your Mind,*' by Avant, making everything seem easier.

"Look, here go a sample and my number, 'cause I know that you gonna like that," I said.

Weed wasn't the most popular drug in the strip club but everybody had to have it on G.P.

She came back like, "That girl, Destiny, over there want to holla at you." And she ended up buying a half ounce with all singles.

"What up? I heard you got good?" Destiny said.

"Naw, I heard that *you* got good. I seen how them niggas was trying to get to you," I said, making her blush.

I was talking shit, but for real she was a stallion. Shorty was light skin with long black curly hair that gave her a Dominican look. She stood about 5'10" with her Gucci heels, and she was already smoking a cigarillo. Standing there with her knees bent inward, it made her legs look bowlegged. The way she was standing made her ass look fatter than it already was.

Even though she wasn't on stage, she still had a natural bounce and a sensual look on her face; swaying back and forth with a dance hall kinda swag. Pulling on her red triple string thong, with her navel pierced, lip pierced, licking them and playing with her tongue ring, eyes low and glazed, she moved as if she was in her own zone; focused on me but rolling to the music at the same time.

Baby was thick to death, with some bright ass baguettes on at least six of her fingers that shined even in the dark. On top of that she had some exotic pearls on that showed off her simple side, smelling like fruit and fruity weed-with a tattoo on her back that had a wave of water with fire on the other side with the Earth centered in the middle and 'Destiny' in cursive on her lower back. Mommy was fine as wine, so keeping my composure was my main concern at this point.

"How much for a half ounce?"

"It's usually three hundred dollars, but since you out shaking, making moves, grinding, just give me two hundred fifty," I said.

And she did. With all singles.

"Black, how much tree we got left?"

I found him at a table back in the corner. Man, this nigga's dizzy and wasn't paying attention worth shit, 'cause that bad ass bitch, Monae, all on his lap.

"Black," I said again. I slid into the seat next to him.

"What's up, Man?" Black said, like I had interrupted something.

"Man, how much tree is we working with?"

"An ounce and a half," Black answered.

The girl, Cinnamon, had just left the stage. She switched over to us and said that she wanted an ounce.

"For you? Give me five hundred." She shot it to me. I had made well over the profit that I was supposed to make.

India said, "next time you better splurge out since I'm in here helping you make all this money." She gave me a hug and kiss on the neck.

She didn't know that I would have been set that cash out. But I wasn't trying to attract too much attention, 'cause *you never know* who was up in there. And I ain't got the strap on me either.

I handed India some money. "Go get me a double of orange-cranberry and Goose and go head and throw the change in the air," I said.

"You want me to throw thirty dollars in the air?" India said, smacking her lips like that was the corniest thing that she ever heard.

"Thirty dollars? Ma, look at what you got," I said. It was about $1,500, all hundreds, so it made the stack look thin.

"As matter-of-fact, bring my nigga a drink, too," I said, thinking this is a night to remember.

India changed the hundreds for singles and started throwing money up in the air, pointing to us, letting the girls know where it had come from.

Shiiit, $1,500 on a Tuesday night at the strip club; that was better than average. I looked at my phone and I had like nine missed calls. We were on our way out the door when Sapphire ran up and said, "Eh Tee, I need two zones for my Jamaican friend. He said that he loves that weed and he'll spend all day if the ticket's right."

"Shiiit, I ain't really doing shit else tonight," I said, feeling a little tired from the long day.

"He said that he'll pay full price for whatever he get," Sapphire said, "Tee." I corrected her.

"It's Ta, Bay. Eh look, call my phone and I'ma meet you at the Den. That's the spot where they sell the gyros," I said.

"I'm hip to it. Yeah I know exactly where that's at," Sapphire said.

"I'm only doing this for you 'cause you're sexy baby," I said, causing Sapphire to put her hands in front of her face for a second so nobody could see her blush from the compliment.

"Call in about twenty-five minutes. Thirty at the latest. And you gone have to be there 'cause I got some things to take care of. Bet?" I said.

"Okay, bet," replied Sapphire.

# Chapter 22

We shot to the house and got the weed. I told Black that we'll do Auntie's house tomorrow. "Yeah, I'm tired too," Black said, yawning.

"You tired? I thought that you was just still stuck from that dance Monae gave you," I said.

"Yeah, right. She ain't have me all like that," Black said, trying to keep a straight face on.

"Hello, is this Tee?"

"Yeah, it's me."

"Yeah, this is Sapphire. Okay, I'ma be there in five minutes. We had to drive slow 'cause friendlies out here crazy," she said.

"Alright, that's cool. I'll be here," I said as I was opening the door up.

"Man, Blizzy, I'm 'bout to go grab a gyro. You want something out of here?" I said.

"Yeah, get me a gyro and tell them to dice up the tomatoes, no onions, with the slightly roasted bread, Swiss cheese instead of American, and oh yeah, tell them I want some ranch fries but put the ranch on the side," Black said.

"Man, that's too much shit to remember, my dude; so you gone have to bring yo ass in," I said.

The cashier said, "One gyro box with cheese eggs."

The girl in front of us got her food then put three dollars in the "Help the People in Haiti Trust Fund" box to help out their foundation.

Me and Black ordered and the lady gave us our change and looked at me but I just put the change right in my pocket. I had gotten so lost in the grind that I had got bullheaded. I started to think that the world was just full of niggas like me, straight hustlers, so when the crisis in Haiti was taking place, that change box looked me directly in my face, but I thought that box was another hustle too. Shiiit. I ain't never been over there so why should I give them people some money? That shit could be a scheme for all I know. Right? Right? Right? Right? That was echoing through my head. Wrong. 'Cause see God was giving me a chance to do some good out of all of the bad that I was doing. And when you slip on doing God's good deeds, then that's when disaster comes and believe me it came.

We had just sat down to wait for our food when my phone rang.

"Hello." It was Sapphire telling me she was there.

"Yeah, what kind of car is you in?" I asked as I walked out the door of the restaurant. She told me and I spotted them. I jumped in the car, getting in the back seat.

Sapphire said, "Ta, this is Fabian. Fabian, Ta. See Ta, I got your name right, this time," she said.

She looked better in her street clothes than she looked in her stage wear. Yeah, she was fine, but she was snorting coke while we was conducting business.

"Ta, do you party?" Sapphire asked as she tooted another line.

I didn't, but I said, "yeah, but I'll pass tonight 'cause I gots to get up early tomorrow morning," I nodded. "Good looking, doe," I said, on the play off side 'cause you never want to make a customer feel awkward.

"That's cool," she said, sniffing and wiping her nose.

"Yeah, I gots to charge you six hundred, then the prices will go down as soon as this next batch comes in. You hear me?" I said this with my usual calm hustling voice; laid back, but still in hustle mode.

"Can I call you?" Fabian asked.

"We'll, right now, you can just have Sapphire call me. She'll give you the number the next time we link," I said, giving Fabian some dap before he got out the ride.

Black came out with the food. "I got yo girl something too. That's where you're going right?' Black asked.

"Yeah, good looking," I said, smiling from feeling like we could go anywhere we want to go with the type of money we were making."

"Black, put one in the air for a night capper," I said, after getting in the car.

We blazed up the square, cruising, doing the speed limit and then, guess who pulled up right behind us? Not one, not two, not three, but four cars deep. Black jumped on the phone quick and called Saree. "Bay, I just got yanked on by the po-po. Where's the registration? In the glove? Alright, I got it and don't worry 'bout shit 'cause I ain't dirty right now."

Black stopped so I could pour the wet out, but they was at the window before I got the chance to throw the bottles. When I tried to tuck them they already had their flashlights and straps on me. 'Damn! These bitches a fuck up a wet dream,' I thought.

"What's the problem, officer?" Black asked.

"Where are you guys coming from?" asked one of the officers.

"We coming from the strip club and getting something to eat," Black clearly explained to the officer.

"Well, the problem is you were swerving. Have you been drinking, young man?" Asked the Italian looking police with the thick black mustache.

"Yeah, I'ma little tired and I have been drinking a little bit but I'm far from drunk," Black answered.

I'm looking at Black, shaking my head, like 'please don't piss them off 'cause I got this paraphernalia on me.'

"Why don't you have on your seat belts?"

"I just took it off. But hey…, what the hell am I getting pulled over for?" Black said, answering a question with a question.

"Hey! You keep your hands up," said one of the officers.

"And by the way, whose car is this?" another officer said while he was pointing his gun at the window, looking stiff in a routine type stand.

"Man, this is my girlfriend's car. The registration is right here. And she's on the phone right now. If you want I can put her on speaker phone right now," Black said, reaching for the phone on his lap.

"No! Don't fucking move!"

"Damn," Black said. "They acting like we killed somebody. Man, here's my license, and here's my insurance. So could you write me a ticket so I can go?"

"Yes, check social security number," an officer said.

I looked over at Black. "Man, I'm going down."

"For what? Fuck you mean you going down?"

"Man, I still got this dumb ass bottle on me. Just come get me out asap."

I swear that I couldn't move. They had straps and lights all in my face the whole time.

'Fuck it. It's only a possession case,' I thought.

I was praying that everything came back clean.

The officer came back to the car yelling, "GET OUT THE CAR!"

"Get the fuck out the car!" yelled the other officer while running up on the car.

"Get out the car? Damn what the fuck I do?" Black asked.

"I'm not going to ask you again. Now get the fuck out the car," he repeated slowly.

He searched the shit out of me first, and pulled $4,600 out of my pockets along with the receipt with the girl, Sofia's name and number on it.

"Hey, you always roll loaded like this? What do you do? Sell drugs out here?" the officer asked.

"Man, I just came from the casino," I answered.

Luckily, the Jamaican girl who gave me the number to buy the tree wrote the number on the receipt for the drinks. "Motor Casino 10:04p.m." with the date to go with it.

"See I told you officer," I said, but he kept searching and that's when he found that bottle.

"Jackpot!" He was waving the bottle back and forth like he had found a kilo or something. But unfortunately for me, it was still enough to take me in.

"Yeah, that's mine, sir. My friend doesn't have anything to do with it. He didn't even know that I had that on me," I explained to the cop.

"It doesn't matter, you're both going to jail."

"Man, I'm not high or drunk, so what am I going to jail for? He just told you that the shit ain't mine," Black said, flipping out on the officers.

"Look! You're going down for intoxication, plus driving without a seatbelt on. Now, do you want to add resisting to that? 'Cause if not, I think you should shut your fucking mouth," yelled the officer.

Still, that was an illegal search, and then I started to thinking that girly from the club might had set me up.

"Damn, my fault, Blizzy. I shouldn't have got caught with that bottle," I said, shaking my head.

"Man, don't sweat that shit. These cocksuckas just wanted to fuck with some niggas," Black said loud, to make sure the cop in the front seat heard him.

"Man, can you tell me exactly what we're going down for?" Black asked.

"Don't worry. If you guys are telling the truth then you should be out by tomorrow," one of the officers said.

"C.O., what's my bond?" I asked, as soon as they stepped in the police station. But the CO said that we didn't have a bond yet, and that we were under investigation.

"Investigation for what?" I asked, calmly.

"Investigation for murder," said the correction officer.

"Man, quit playing. This gots to be a joke," I said.

"Naw, for real," the CO said. "The detectives wants to talk to you in the morning, so sleep tight."

"Man, I hope Saree called my girl and let her know what's up."

"Fuck it," he said. "We'll be out tomorrow-then tomorrow it is."

"Black, what up bohhy?" I asked.

"Ain't shit up. I'm 'bout to lay this shit on down, 'cause we'll be out tomorrow and this shit don't stop, ya heard?" Black said, sounding exhausted from a hard night.

# Chapter 23

"Nine in the morning came, and a breakfast tray was sitting there. I could hear the CO's keys shaking.

"Yeah, somebody wants to see you," the CO said.

"CO, did I get a bond yet?"

"Not yet," he said, closing my cell, making sure that it was shut and secure. "Come this way."

I went in the room with two detectives. Funny thing is they looked like rock stars in suits more than they looked like detectives.

"Tashawn Adams, it seems like you've been keeping your nose clean lately."

"Yeah, for a few years to be exact," said one of the detectives, looking through a folder that was on the desk.

"Well, let me get straight to the point. Somebody told me that you did not get along with Mr. Austin."

"Who the fuck is Mr. Austin?" I asked with both of my hands in the air like I was clueless.

"Look, don't play stupid with me boy. A guy gets found shot to death, butt naked and some people said that you and him don't get along."

"The man's name was Rino," said the second detective, busting into the conversation."

"Oh snap! Rino's dead?" I acted shocked.

"You know he's dead, Tashawn. You know he's fucking dead," said the first detective, looking at me with an angry look, trying to shake me up.

"Naw, with all honesty, sir; I didn't really like that guy, and we exchanged some harsh words before, but it was never deep enough to kill that man."

I was sitting there thinking about what I had heard about him getting merked and thinking who did it, and that I knew I wouldn't have wasted a bullet on that nigga.

"Somebody told us that you and your friend, Kenny..., your brother, your dude, Kenneth, or whoever the fuck he is to you, was last seen with him," the detective said.

See right here, I could put myself in the mix, 'cause somebody could of told them that, but I doubt it, so I gots to go all the way street.

"Who is Kenneth?" I asked with a smirk on my face, looking cool and poised.

"So, you're telling me that you don't know who you was riding with?" the first detective asked, slamming his fist on the table. "You guys call him Black," the detective yelled at me.

"Man, I was out of town and I told you that. I don't know nothing 'bout nothing. You can send my condolences to his family, but really, this shit ain't got nothing to do with me. Matter fact, you can send me back to my cell," I said, looking at the detective straight in his eyes. I didn't blink one time. "I need to get my thoughts together anyway," I said.

"Yeah, you know yo' man, Black is gonna give you up," the second detective said.

"I know. But do one thing for me. Just tell him to keep my books tight, alright?" I said.

"Okay smart ass. We're gonna see how smart you are when you're in Lucasville maximum security," one of the detectives said.

They couldn't get shit out of me and one wrong word or move and they woulda seriously put something on me.

"Kenneth Rogers, that your name, right? A.K.A., Black, right?" said the first detective.

Black just stared at them.

"Now, I just had a nice conversation with Ta, and you know he's gonna give you up, so you might wanna make it light on yourself," the detective added. "Tell me what happened."

"He gone give me up for a seatbelt ticket? That's fucked up," Black said, smiling like he wasn't worried at all.

"Oh that's what you think you're in here for? Boy you must think this shit is a joke," the second detective said.

"You wanna play dumb, or do you want to tell me who killed Larino Austin?" said the detective.

"Oh, I guess this is the part where I'm supposed to be like, 'Oh detective, I know who did it, and I'll tell you everything, just don't put me in jail,' right?" Black said sarcastically. "But check this out. I don't know who killed Larino and I really don't give a fuck. So you can get your hot ass coffee breath out of my fucking face and send me back to my cell."

"You're a tough guy, huh? Well, we'll see how tough you are with all those felonies you got. And I'll make sure that your tough ass never sees daylight again," said the detective. He was frustrated from getting zero information out of either of his suspects.

"Man, send me back to my fucking cell, NOW," Black said so loud that it echoed like a lion's roar.

Shiit, my seventy-two hour investigation was up. Yeah, this was the third day being locked up. Technically, they could use up to another forty-eight hours, an extension to find more evidence.

"C.O. What up? I got a bond yet?" I asked, standing up with my head resting in between the jail bars. "What's up? Check Adams for me," I added.

"No bond, Adams, but I was about to tell you that they're giving you two a straight release."

Forty-eight more hours wasn't needed because that receipt with Sofia's name and number on it had the time and date on it too. So basically our stories matched and it put me and Black in the clear. And just to make sure, they checked the video tape, and we was right there like we said we was, at the time when Rino came up dead. Straight release, no tickets, no bond, and no fines.

No apologies either, but I ain't emotional. Shiit, just let me the fuck out, right? Plus, it didn't hurt that our girls were constantly calling, checking on us. I couldn't wait to see Felicia. But I knew I was gone have some explaining to do, especially when she found out her friend Rino was dead.

We stepped outside the Justice Center and the feeling of freedom pretty much made us forget everything that we had just went through. It was like bringing the dead back alive.

"Black, give me a light," I said. "Man, that shit was crazy," I added. "I wonder who did that shit?" I dug into my pockets searching for a lighter.

"Shiit, It ain't got nothing to do with us, so fuck it," Black said.

"Man, let me get a light real quick. Didn't you have one in your property?" I said. I was getting frustrated. I needed to smoke.

"Oh, yeah. Here. Damn, my nigga, you still got that square?" Black asked.

"Hell yeah, bohhy. I had to tuck him, you know that. I wasn't 'bout to let them take the last of the last," I said.

"You a fool, man," Black said, laughing. "A damn fool."

We started blowing the square that I had tucked before friendly had pulled up on us. It was dry before I lit it but when I put a flame to it, it got right back oily.

"Shiit, let me hit that, man," Black said.

"Man, hold up a second," I said.

"Come on, man. You had it when we got pulled over," Black said.

"Damn, nigga, here. Calm down, doe, and quit fiending." I said it like a joke but I was lightweight serious.

"Man, never fiending," Black said. He got his composure back.

"Here comes yo girl," I said, seeing her car pull up.

Saree rolled down the window. "Felicia said she'll be here in five minutes."

"I know. I just hollered at her," I said.

"So, y'all gone stay out the way, right?" Saree asked.

"Yeah, you know it," I said. Black passed the square back.

"Yeah, man. I'm 'bout to go hop in the shower, eat some real food, and get dressed. Shiit, so what time is you gone be ready?" Black asked.

"About three hours, 'cause I'm 'bout to do the same thing. So, we'll link in a minute."

"Alright, in a minute. Bet." We gave each other dap then parted.

Saree blew the horn before she pulled off. She said, "Y'all gone stay out them strip clubs, too, right?"

*Damn how she know that*? I thought. Oh yeah, I remembered. Saree was on the phone when the police officers had asked where we were coming from. And Black said, "We're coming from the strip club and getting something to eat, sir." So then most likely, Saree told Felicia on me.

## Chapter 24

Felicia pulled up in her new Honda Accord with tinted windows. "Ta, come on." I still couldn't wait to see her. *Brvoom! Brvoom! Brvoom!*

She was blowing the horn crazy at this girl that had her kids in the car with her that was backing up.

"Damn, here I come, Ma. I know you can't wait to see me, but damn," I said, trying to break the tension.

I could tell that she was frustrated 'cause she was mad already but her driving skills were average because Felicia didn't drive that much. She had just got her license earlier that year. I jumped in the car.

"You know I hate coming down here, Ta. It's never nowhere to park," Felicia said, scolding me.

I leaned over to give her a kiss. She showed a slight hesitation at first, then gave me a quick kiss.

"Ta, you stink," she said, with her face squinted up.

"I know, Ma. I gots to jump in the shower asap, and I'm hungry, too," I said

She was driving, blowing the horn crazy at people, so I could tell that something was bothering her. Soon as I was about to ask what was wrong, she turned toward me, looking at me with a face my mother used to make at me, and for a minute, that's who it felt like I was riding with again.

"So how did you manage to get high already, and you just got out of jail five minutes ago?" she asked. But it was like her mouth was moving but my mother's voice was coming out. *"Tashawn, how did you manage to get suspended in your last period of class?"*

"What about this strip club shit?" Felicia was still talking. "I guess that episode that we had in the park earlier that day wasn't good enough for you, huh?" she said.

But instead, I heard my mother saying, *"And why is you stealing lunch tokens? I guess all that good stuff that I packed in your lunch box wasn't good enough for you?"*

I said the words to Felicia, but it felt like I was answering my mother. *"Naw, Mom. It ain't like that."*

"Yeah, I guess Ta got all the women flocking him 'cause he stay serving and swerving and flipping cars. And I guess you and your compadre," she turned and looked at me; "yeah, you and yo' nigga, Black, yeah, I guess y'all just supposed to be the next Gotti and Capone."

"Naw, it ain't like that, Ma," I said, shaking my head, not really able to get a word out because I was tripping on the conversation being like with my mom.

*"And when I worked second shift the other day, what's this I hear about you hanging in front of the mini park all night? I guess you and yo' little friends is thugs now, huh? I guess you outgrew yo' football, huh?"* I heard my mother say.

"I wonder if one of them little stripper hoes called the police station for three days in a row 24/7." Felicia's lips were moving fast. She pointed her finger at me. "I'm calling, trying to see if you had a bond__or I guess I'm just dumb for worrying about you all night?"

*" I guess you just want to make me look like a bad mother all around the table, Tashawn."* My mother was pointing her finger at me just like Felicia was doing.

*"Tashawn, boy, I swear you messing up yo' life already. You about to be on punishment, boy, and you're gonna be in the house for a long time."*

*"But mom . . ."*

*"What, boy? Don't interrupt me when I'm talking to you."*

*"Yeah, but here, Mom. I found three hundred dollars. But I don't need it 'cause I still got that twenty dollars that grandma gave me. So here, Mom. I want you to have it."*

*"Tashawn, how did you find three hundred dollars? People don't just find that kinda money."*

*"I know, but see when I got suspended I was sad, so I was walking with my head down, and at first I thought it was just a dollar but it was three hundred."*

*"Tashawn, go play football, but don't be out all day. Wait boy. Promise me that you'll do your homework first," my mother said.*

*"I promise, Mom."*

I held my head in my hands. I had both of these women in my head at the same time. I shook my head hard. I was back then with moms, and couldn't handle it. So how was I gonna handle this shit with Felicia?

"Ta, that's what I'm saying about you coming home every night. Rino's dead. You're in the street. What if the same type of shit happens to you?" Felicia said, with tears falling from her eyes. "It's plenty of men out here. So why did I have to fall in love with Tashawn Adams?" She wiped the tears from her eyes. "Ta, I can't take this. You ain't even gone say nothing?" She turned and looked at me. "You're selfish and you make me sick with that *I don't give a fuck attitude*," Felicia said.

Girly was pissed, so I had to think quick 'cause this was going too far.

"Ma, I came up on a few extra dollars at the casino." I reached down in my pocket. "Since we weren't charged, we got all our property back. 'Cause see that's where we really were. This is what I had put to the side for you," I said, handing Felicia a knot of money.

"Ta, you can't just give me money every time you do something wrong," Felicia said with tears still flowing down her face.

"But, Bay. You ain't even count it yet. Alright it's three thousand dollars. I want you to go do something nice for yo'self. Alright?... because I love you and I was on my way to you before I had got picked up by friendly and company," I said.

"I love you, too," Felicia said, as if the amount of money just stopped her tears instantly.

"Oh, pull up here so I can grab a milkshake. Don't you want a root beer float, Ma?" I asked.

"Yes Ta," Felicia said, as if she had got defeated by the combination of love and money.

The money that I gave her put her straight on hush mode. See, I knew that girly wasn't all about the money; she proved that already, but she's a part of my life now, and I can't have her tripping on me; not a teeny bit while I'm on this grind. But three Gs out the blue a warm up any females heart. But for my girl, I figured that it was well worth it.

"I'm sorry about your friend, Rino," I said.

"That's so sweet, Ta, considering that y'all ain't really like each other. Ta, promise me if you go out with Black, that you'll be safe and come home," she said, while she was rubbing the back of my head.

"You mean come see you?" I asked. "Cause I thought that I lived by myself."

"Ta, you know what I mean," Felicia muttered, in her soft voice. That was one of the things that made her irresistible to me.

"Alright, Ma. I promise."

"Ta, I want you to come to my house with me for a minute." She licked her lips in a flirty type of way.

"Ma, I would, but I stink, doe. And I been in these same clothes for the last three days," I said.

"I know, crazy. Look in the trunk. I got you a few things."

I went to the trunk and pulled out three bags. We went into the house and I opened all the bags up like it was Christmas.

One bag had a box with some retro Bo Jackson, white and gray. In the other bag, it was some exclusive Polo jeans and three crispy white Ts, plus a polo robe with the pockets on the side of it. Then she hit me off with the thin hoodie and a white and gray Indians fitted to match the kicks, new boxer shorts and socks, Lever 2000 soap, plus some Vaseline and two different kinds of toothpaste, some Degree deodorant, some body wash, Ax body spray, a pack of razors that I probably will never use, some baby powder and some African Pride hair grease. Oh yeah, Gucci cologne, some Lagerfeld, Curve, and some other type oils and some Fahrenheit that she must'a smelled on me before-for her to know that I was into that. There was some new face towels and big towels, some dental floss and some whitening strips for a nigga's choppers.

"Ma, where did you get all this stuff from? And what you got, a booster or something?" I asked. I was in complete shock at all the stuff she got for me.

"No, Ta. Not everybody be in the streets," Felicia said. I didn't know exactly what you liked, so I tried to get a variety. All this stuff is corny, huh?" she asked, seemingly hesitant.

"Naw. Hell naw!" I said. "Ma, it's perfect. And even more than what I deserve."

"Thanks, Boo. Anything for you," she said, in a bashful way.

So I went back to Felicia's house with her and jumped straight in the shower. After that I laid up with her and we watched some smack DVDs then got dressed. I sat back on the couch and checked my messages.

# Chapter 25

*"You have sixteen new messages and four saved messages,"* came out the phone in a computerized voice.

*"New message sent Wednesday at 2am.* 'Oh, I see how y'all nigga's playing. Yeah nigga, I got you, doe. It's SOS, my nigga, and that's on the Bricks. I got y'all niggas." *Beeep. Message erased.*

*"Next message sent Wednesday 2:48am.* Eh, what up nephew? This is Auntie. I was just a little worried about you, sweetheart. Call me if y'all still out and about. Okay. Bye." *Beeep. Message erased. "New message, Wednesday 10:03am.* "Ta, what's going on? This is Will right here. I just wanted to let you know that I'll be home no later than Saturday."

*Damn! I almost forgot about Will*, I thought, as I was flipping through my phone.

*"New message sent Wednesday at 10:09am.* "Man, you a hard cat to catch up with. Eh, get wit me, doe. This Luth. You know the number."

*Beeep. Message erased.*

*"New message sent Wednesday at 10:45am.* Hello. Yeah. Hey hun. What are you doing? This is Ronisa, boy. Y'all missing all kinda action; oops, I mean all these video games. Call back when you get this message." *Beeep message erased.*

*"New message. Message skipped."*

*"New message sent Thursday at 12pm.* "Man, what's up, Sucka? This Luth right here, bohhy. I been calling yo phone for the last two days, nigga. If you scared, just say you is and you know where to go."

"Man, shut yo fat ass up, Luth," I said, talking back to the message, shaking my head, laughing.

*"New message sent Thursday at 1:31pm.* Man, nigga, what's up? This Lil' Man, bitch ass nigga. You already know what it is, nigga. Shoot on site, bitch!"

*Beeep message erased. "You have no more messages."*

Felicia stepped in the room right before I turned the speaker off. "Ta, who was that?" asked Felicia, standing over me while I was sitting on the couch with her hands on her hips.

I put my hand around her waist and replied, "that was nobody."

"Well, that nobody didn't sound too friendly," Felicia said, while she sat on my lap.

"Don't worry 'bout it, Ma. Come here," I said, as I started kissing her on the lips. "Anyway, who needs friends when I got you," I said.

"Okay. I get it. You can go hang out with yo' nigga, Black," Felicia said.

"Aahhh! I need permission now? Well, look Boo, you gots to drop me off to my whip 'cause I ain't riding in that hot ass Jeep."

"Ta, damn. I gots to do my little cousin, Monique's hair. Here go the keys. Could you just take my car, please? I don't have anywhere to go and the only thing that I gots to do this week is take care of you, my king." Then she added, "If I'm gone, then here's a key to the house. We might be gone for a minute if it's crowded at the mall or these plazas."

"A key?" I said, looking somewhat confused.

"Yes, Ta, and just because I'm giving you a key to my house doesn't mean that I'm asking you for a key to yours."

"Naw. I ain't say that, Bay," I said. I leaned over and kissed her on the lips. Man, this girl is trying to lock me down and I ain't even mad at it.

My phone interrupted the moment.

"Hello. Hello," I said. I couldn't hear through the bad reception. "Hello?"

"Yeah. Can you hear me?" It was Will.

"Yeah. A little bit. But it sound like this bitch keep going in and out," I said.

"Look. I'll be there for sure tomorrow," Will said.

"Eh, Will? You think I can get the exact same model of car that you got?"

"Well, I realize that I'm getting old__and that car might not be for me. So I was thinking about selling you that one," Will said. "Now that's a might, so we'll talk about it when I get back," he added.

"Alright. I'll see you tomorrow," I said.

"What?"

"I said I'll holler at you tomorrow." The bad reception was frustrating me.

"Alright. Bet."

"Hello?" I clicked over. My phone stayed hot.

"Black, what's up?" I said.

"Hello. Yeah man, that bitch sounds crazy."

"What you talking about?"

"That phone, my nigga," Black replied.

"I probably gots to dump this puppy," I said.

"Yeah. I'ma gone head and turn this one in too," he said.

"Eh. We need to go holla at yo phone dude asap," I said.

"Yeah, we can do that. I'm ready, doe, right now. What's up? You want me to come swoop, right?" Black asked.

"In the Jeep. Is you craaaazy?" I said. "Where is you at?"

"Over Saree's house."

"What street is that again? Oh never mind. I remember. Alright. I'll be there in about twenty minutes."

"Bet," Black replied.

"Man, I'm ready to go nuts in this bitch. It's time to get some cash, ya heard me? Out of commission for three days? I'll be there in a minute," I said. I put in a Young Jeezy CD. Music motivated me to grind harder.

First I hit the house. In and out to grab the bowling ball bags. Man, I'm loving this whip. This bitch is roomy and it's new, tinted windows, and it smells good like a rental.

I picked up Black and Saree was watching him leave standing in the doorway. I waved and said, "What's up, Saree?" But she gave me a twisted face and slammed the door.

"Damn. What was that about?"

"I don't think she likes you. She only likes me," Black replied. He had a playful grin on his face.

"She'll get over it," I said.

"Naw. She said you get me in trouble for real."

"Aaahh! I get you in trouble? What about you getting me in trouble?"

"Naw, for real, doe. All jokes aside. She said that we're too tight. And that she seen our kind before. She said that we're gonna get in some more shit and then she started crying, saying that she love me and that Ta is a real nice person too. She said she don't want to see nothing bad happen to us and all this and that," Black said.

"So what did you say?"

"Shiit. I said $2500."

"What?" I shook my head. I didn't get it.

"You heard me. I said $2500. Here. Now go shopping. Then I put this rod in her life and everything was all roses again."

"Man, you got that shit from me," I said.

"Man, I got that shit. That's all that matters," Black said. He pulled out bands, flossing on the low key side.

Yeah, we figured since we had bust that move on Lil' Man, then the Dale a be kinda hot. That was the last place that I told him to come. So it's possible that they might be leaning on the spot. A nigga ain't really give a fuck. But it was time to straight grind.

Therefore, we ain't need no drama. So we went to the phone spot; then headed straight to the west side.

I changed my voicemail off rip. "Hey, new number. Call 755-5540."

# Chapter 26

"Hello. Are y'all alright?" Ronisa asked. "Is everything everything?"

"Yeah, but we're over Lisa's house. Matter-a-fact, she wants to talk to you," I said. I put it on speaker and handed the phone to Lisa.

"Hey, what's up, girl? Why haven't you been coming around?" Lisa asked. She was filing and blowing on her fingernails.

"Cause you live too far, girl," she said.

"Uhn-uh. Stop acting like that girl. Acting all brand new. Bring yo ass over here 'cause I'm trying to put something in the air," Lisa said.

Everything was falling into play. This way, Ronisa will bring everybody that was calling her phone to Lisa's house.

"Fat Luth, what up?" I said. I dialed him next.

"What's up?" Luth said. "You still good?"

"Yeah, but can you come to the west side?"

"Damn, Ta. You know that my LS is fucked up."

"Alright, then look. I'ma bout to meet you right off the freeway. So be right there by that Plaza," I said.

Everybody on the west side don't complain. That's what I love about it. If they know that they were getting good quality then they were satisfied. Plus, it was all kinda different nationalities over there. So you was bound to see anything over there. The police couldn't pin your moves. Why? Because everything moves fast and it's more easy to blend in. Yeah, we even made a trip and hollad at O a few more times in the mix of all the grind.

Yeah, all I lost was Lil' Man. Other than that, this shit was backed up and running like water.

"Look at these niggas. Some real life ganstas," Lisa commented, pointing at me and Black.

"Oh yeah, girl. You know it," her friend said, co-signing.

I think that the hood think that we really killed Rino. Fuck it. As long as the police knew we didn't do it.

Lisa was a clear liquor drinking, Newport smoking, perfect blunt rolling, weed smoking, sexy woman from the west side. Yeah, she was what we really call west side live. She handles her business but she gets geeked up on a daily.

"Black, here go one hundred dollars. Murder's outside waiting on you to get that bottle," I said.

Sofia called out the blue and said that she was close to Cleveland and that she wanted to come and holler at me if she could. Man, she ain't even know that she was like my guardian angel 'cause if it wasn't for her sliding me that number on the receipt, then we woulda been through, and probably would have still been under investigation.

"Sofia, I'm over my friend's house. I'ma give her the phone so she can give out the directions, alright?" I said. "Eh, here Lisa. I need you to tell my friend how to get here."

"You know I charge for that," Lisa said. She was smoking on her cigarette. "Hello. Yeah? Where are you now, Sweetie?" Lisa asked.

"I'm close to Akron?" Sofia said, sounding as if it was more of a question than an answer.

"Girl, are you Jamaican? I love your accent, girl. You gone have to hook me up with one of your cousins or something. Okay, this is what you do to get here." She gave Sofia the directions.

"We gone have a full house, so I think we better go get something to eat," Lisa said. "I got some extra cash on the card, so do y'all want anything?"

"Oh yeah, grab a few things that we can put on the grill," I said.

"On the grill?" Lisa said, with one hand on her hip. "Don't y'all got women?"

"Ma, just cook something," Black demanded.

"Black, shut up with yo smart ass mouth. Boy, I'ma do it because I'm hungry and I know that Ronisa's hungry too. Star, come on so I can drop you off," Lisa said. She grabbed her car keys off the table and headed for the door.

"Okay. I'm 'bout to run around the corner, and yo' friend said that she'll be here in thirty minutes, but I should be back by then. So, be good while I'm gone, okay?"

Now I got thirty minutes to think and I'm thinking that I need to have a good day 'cause I'm trying to cop this old school from Will.

"Eh yo, Ta, let me holla at you for a minute," Black said.

"Yeah, what's up, Blizzy?" I asked.

"Look, I know that we're on a stack mission, but I love that old school, too. So, man, you think that you can get yo man to get me one too? Just like the one that you're trying to get?" Black asked.

"Yeah. Hell yeah. You know I'll do that for you," I said.

I knew he could tell that was coming from the heart. And I could see me and this nigga would still be locked up if he woulda said anything wrong, but he stayed quiet like he was supposed to.

"Nigga, if I ride schooly then you can too, my nigga. I told you this is P.F.L. – Partners for Life," I said.

"Man, quit saying that shit. That shit is corny, Ta. We gone have to change the name or something," Black said, laughing.

"Man, whatever." I said, waving my hand at Black. "Man, tap something straight out the bottle, nigga."

We dipped the square, then chopped it up about how we was gone rock in the next couple of days. Since we planned on getting these whips, we was gone need every dolla, every quarter, every dime, and every nickel, all the way down to every fucking red cent, ya heard?

Ronisa rolled up in perfect timing, and Lisa pulled up like twenty-five seconds behind her.

"Looking good, girl."

"You too, Sugar."

You could tell that they were happy to see each other, like little childhood friends.

Lisa pointed to me and Black. "You remember the little gangstas, right?"

"Uh-huh." Ronisa nodded her head. "Y'all come over here and give me a hug," she said, talking like we were babies. "I'm glad that y'all is out that place, doe."

"Right, right," I said. Black snuck a kiss on her neck while he was hugging her.

"Boy, look out," Ronisa said, pushing Black away, laughing. They basically treated us like little brothers. That's why it was nothing for me to let Felicia know that this was who I was gone be around while I'm doing my thing.

Ronisa and Lisa was some jazzy, fast paced, but caring women, that didn't have no interest in little gangstas like us. At least that's what they called us. They both had baby fathers that was doing life, one at Lucasville and the other at Mansfield. And the truth of the matter is we *were* little gangstas, but their niggas would probably make us look like pussycats.

"Ta, could you get this grill started for me?" Lisa asked. She was putting things in the refrigerator, always moving fast. "I got these chicken breasts that you asked for. I got some scampi, some T-bone steaks, and some brocks, now tell me I ain't that bitch," Lisa said.

"You already know that you that Queen B," I said, nudging Black with my elbow. They both smiled because he knew I was gassing her up.

"Oh yeah..., Sofia said that she'll be here in five minutes. I love how she talks. Boy, you know that y'all got too many girls."

"That's not my girl. I mean she's cool peoples, you know. And that is my girl but what I'm trying to say is not like that, 'cause see, I'm in love with Felicia," I said.

"Okay. Well I hope that you treat Felicia good. Look Ta, I know that we stay high and drunk and joke around a lot," Lisa said, talking with both hands on my face like a grandmother, "but y'all need to set some goals and make some plans so the two of you can leave this lifestyle alone." She was crying a little bit; I think from being drunk. "Cause see, I don't want to see y'all end up like Javon's father. He ain't never coming home," she said. "And he wasn't even that hard of a nigga," she added, still crying. "I just don't want the same thing to happen to you and yo friend, Black." She wiped tears from her eyes.

"That's my partner, Sweety. And I'm glad that you're concerned about a nigga, but it ain't even bout to be like that, Lisa. See, we ain't doing nothing major, just moving a little green, you know, and everything's gone work out smooth. Alright?" I said.

"You know you're like a little brother to me, Ta. Even though I haven't known y'all for a long time, I still got love for y'all," Lisa said.

"I know, Ma. It's cool. But ain't nobody watching us, so we should be alright," Black said, wiping the rest of her tears off of her face, then giving her a hug, assuring her that we're safe when we're in the streets.

*Call from So-fi-a.* "Eh, hold up y'all. I gots to take this call."

"Hello," I said.

"Yeah, what up, Rude Boy?" Sofia said.

"Damn, Ma. You said five minutes. Hold up. I can't really hear you 'cause somebody's riding bikes through here," I said.

"That somebody is me silly. And I think we're outside," Sofia said.

"You tink?" I asked, making fun of her accent.

"Don't make fun of me boy."

"Ma, you know I'm just playing with you," I said. We shared a laugh.

When I came out to meet her, she was on a black and grey Yamaha R-1000. There were three other riders with her. She said it was her brother and the two girls were her twin cousins, which was obvious because they looked just like each other.

"Ta, this is Antonio, and these are the twins Terry and Teresa," said Sofia, introducing her family to me.

"Hey, where's Black?" she said all of a sudden.

"Black's around. Matter-of-fact he's right over there handling business." I pointed to him.

"Hey, Black," Sofia waved her hand at him. Black threw up his fist then put up one finger as if he was saying, hold up, he'll be over there in a second.

I dapped up her brother first just to make sure he was official.

"What's up my dude? Nice bike," I said.

"Good looking, mon. You ride, too?" Antonio asked.

"Naw, I really don't do the bikes, but I might learn to ride one day," I said.

"Yeah, mon. You should learn. You'll love it."

"What up, doe?" I said, putting on my business face.

"Yeah. I heard good tings about you, mon. I don't know you well but I know that I like dem trees that my sister got from you, and so did my peoples," Antonio said.

"Yo peoples?" I asked.

"Yeah, mon. My peoples from Central State. That's where we go to school. And now we're trying to get these apartments together. No more staying on campus, you feel me?"

"Oh yeah! Y'all go to college, huh? Well that's what's up." I felt proud of them for doing something positive. But the thought of them going to school got me stuck for a second. I hadn't met a lot of hustlers trying to get a degree.

"Oh there's Black, Sofia," I said.

Black walked toward us. He must have finished his business.

"Hey Black," Sofia said. She seemed happy to see him.

"Hey, girl. What's up? Why you just standing there girl? Come give me a hug."

"I see you over there still chasing that dough, bohhy," Sofia said, trying to make fun of the way we say "boy."

"You already know; I'm from the Bricks," Sofia said, as she jumped in before Black said it. We all laughed but her family didn't really get it. But it was an inside thing from the night Black was clowning at the casino.

"Y'all had to be there," Black said. He gave Antonio some dap and gave the twins hugs.

"Eh, y'all going in, right? We got some things on the grill," I said.

"Ta, quit trying to talk like me," Sofia said.

"Alright, mon."

She laughed, then punched me in my arm.

"Naw look, doe, there's Lisa. She's gonna take you in so y'all can get something to eat and drink," I said.

"Hey Lisa." Sophia smiled as she walked over.

"Giirl, I love yo voice. Come on in and talk to me. And who are these beautiful girls right here?" Lisa asked.

"These are my cousins," Sofia said. She seemed to be amused by Lisa's good energy.

"Hey babies," Lisa said. "I used to look like that twenty years ago. They are some dolls."

"Oh, by the way, this is Ronisa."

"Hey y'all," Ronisa said. She rolled up, already chinky-eyed from the first blunt.

Antonio stayed outside with me and Black.

"Hold on honey."

## Chapter 27

The phone was still a big part of my hustle even though the hand-to-hand was killing it.

"What's up Luiz? What was you trying to do?" I asked.

"A quarter ounce."

"Bet. That a be one hundred twenty-five dollars for you, my dude."

"Amigo, you killing me," Luiz said.

"Come on, Holmes. What you want me to do? I already took twenty-five dollars off, so show yo nigga some love," I said.

Alright, most people who complained was gonna spend anyway. They just liked hearing themselves talk. Or they wanted to hear me talk, and I didn't mind compromising and negotiating myself. It made me feel like I was working, at least. "Hey, Sara, what's up?" I said.

"Ta, you wouldn't believe what I just went through all day. This and that, that and this. Even my fucking boss was tripping. At this point, I just wanna go home and rollup and smoke. Then sit on a fat cock. Here's two hundred dollars, Ta. Can I please get a quarter," Sara said.

Shiit, she threw the price out there so I jumped on it. Even a hustla deserves a tip every now and then.

This bitch was going now. Everybody had came out for a second; let's just say a mini rush came.

Everybody from Arabs, "Look my friend, I need two ounces. I got a nice girl with me."

Them niggas always got one of our hood rats with them, but they don't never bring their little bitches out. The groupies were out too. A group of chicks rolled up four deep. "Hey Ta. Hey Black. We love y'all," said a car full of groupie chicks. And groupie was sugarcoating things 'cause when it came down to it, they were just ordinary blunt berries. "So can we smoke?"

"Hell yeah, you can. For ten dollars," Black said, laughing. He dapped me up. "Pirating," we said together.

Old people even came through during the rush.

"Yeah, let me get a fifty sack, man," John J said.

"John J, what the fuck is a fifty sack?"

"Well, here just give me however many joints I supposed to get for fifty dollars and hurry up because y'all young niggas bout to make me late to the Drink and Drown."

Everybody was coming, and a nigga had to get all of that money from everybody that came to us. Everybody but the ones that was too young.

"Eh, my dude. Let me get a motherfucking ounce," said the young hustla.

"My little nigga, you know that's gone run you about five hundred," I said. Young'un pulled like two bands out his pocket and handed it to me.

"That's five hundred. So what's up?" he said. "Count it out if you want to," he added.

"Man, hold up. Let me see some I.D.," I said.

"Man, I'm eighteen."

"I don't know. Black how old do you think this little muthafucka is?"

"Yeah, my nigga. We might need to see yo I.D.," Black said.

"See my I.D.? What the fuck? Y'all niggas the police or something? Y'all want to see a nigga's government. Man, let me get my weed so I can be out," the young'un said. He looked at his phone like he was missing licks on account of me messing with him.

Man, I don't know what Auntie was talking bout; saying, "Y'all niggas ain't about that paper for real."

I looked at Black and he shrugged his shoulders like, whatever.

"Man, here. One ounce. Now get yo little ass up out of here," I said.

After the rush, we chopped it up with Antonio, Sofia's brother.

"Alright. What's up with you, man?" I asked.

"I just wanted something small right now. I ain't really got it like y'all," Antonio said. "But I do want to grab a quarter pound from y'all, doe."

"Yeah, since you're Sofia's brother-then I'll let you get it for $1,600 even," I said.

"Ta, y'all come get these plates before y'all food gets cold," Ronisa called out to us.

"Antonio, do you drink?" Lisa asked.

"On occasion," he replied.

"Well, I got Patron and some Red Stripe, so let me know, Hun," Lisa said. The way Lisa was looking, I was surprised she had any alcohol left to offer a nigga. She must've been drinking the whole time she was cooking. She sho' wasn't like that when we first got there.

My phone rang just as we were all getting our plates.

"Hello," I said.

"What's up, bohhy?" Felicia said.

"Shiit. Nothing. Thinking 'bout you," I said. "You sound amped up, Ma."

"I am," Felicia said. "And thanks again for them dollars you gave me, Boo. Ta?"

"Yeah. What's up, Bay?"

"Do you got some more of them quarters? The funny squares?" she asked.

"Oh yeah?" I knew she had to be feeling good 'cause she was trying to smoke.

"Bay," I said. "I thought that you wasn't smoking no more."

"Ta, pleeese?" Felicia asked in the voice that I could never say 'no' to. "I'll wear my trench coat, too," she laughed. "I remember how you looked when I opened it up that day in the park."

"Damn, Ma. You gone hit a nigga with the voice and the trench too? That was a low blow," I said, smiling. I was enjoying the conversation.

"Oh, and Saree and my cousin, Monique, is trying to holla at y'all on the one thing," she said.

"Hold up, Boo," I said. I put the phone down. "Eh, Black. Saree said that she's trying to come holla at you for some weed."

"Shiiit, tell her to come on then," Black said.

"Yeah, come on," I said, talking back into the phone. "You remember where I'm at right?"

"Kinda," she said. "I'll call if I get lost. Smooches."

We were all eating and drinking and playing spades, listening to Lisa's new system with the music on low.

"So y'all gone ride them bikes all the way back to Central State tonight?" Lisa asked.

"No, girl. That's way too far. And you best believe, it's too late. We done rented some rooms at dat big hotel downtown, the Hilton," Sofia said, barely getting it out from her strong accent.

"Really? The Hilton is a lovely place," Lisa said.

"Not as lovely as how decorated dis place," Sofia said. She looked around the room. "And girl, I love dis fish tank."

"Aww girl, you just saying that. Now how old is your brother? And is he into older women?" Lisa asked. She was a little tipsy.

"Who? Antonio? Girl, he don't know what he likes yet. He's still wet behind the ears." She gave Lisa a high five.

"Ta, grab that ranch dressing for me," Black said.

"Yeah Antonio; fuck with me, doe, and shit a get better, ya dig? Hold up. Hello," I said, answering the phone, wiping my mouth with a napkin.

"Ta, which one of these apartments is hers?" It was Felicia.

"The third one, Boo."

"Okay, then I'm outside," she said. "I want you to come out, Ta. I want to show you something."

I'm wondering what got her all geeked up. Me and Black went outside and Felicia had on a chain and matching bracelet with champagne diamonds in it, and Saree had the same set on.

I'm like, "Damn Monique, why didn't you light up?"

She was smirking. "Well, you know I'm lightweight too young for all that right now." She smiled at me with her teeth showing her new grill. It was all platinum with white diamonds in it.

"Damn," I said. I was digging her grill. That shit was shining.

"Bay, we making these hoes tuck and roll ain't we?" Felicia asked.

"Yeah, y'all fucked them up with that move that y'all put down," I said in admiration. "Oh yeaaah."

"Y'all stunting out like that? Man that's what's up," Black said. "Y'all got little cuz on it too?"

"Yeah, looking all cute and fly," I added.

"Ta, shut up," Monique said, smiling. She seemed a little embarrassed but still smiling, showing off her new mouthpiece.

Saree and Felicia both moved like they were synchronized and Monique was their young henchman.

"Ta, give us a square. Wait hold up. Saree you still gone smoke with me?" Felicia asked. She seemed to want to make sure that she didn't have to smoke by herself. Saree nodded. "Alright, Ta, come on give us a square," she said.

"Damn, Ma, you feeling real good tonight, huh?"

"You know it, Baby," Felicia said, kissing me on the lips. She leaned up against the car.

I don't like mixing business with pleasure but I didn't want to seem like I was hiding something 'cause if the relationship's not right, then the grind definitely won't be right. Then it comes out to that we might as well not even be together.

They smoked and regained their composure and came and joined the cookout. The girls walked in looking each other up and down, complimenting each other's outfits and jewelry. Ronisa introduced everybody for me, which made it easier.

"Girl, I love that purse, and where did you get those diamonds from?" Ronisa asked.

"Oooh child, and yo little mouth looks beautiful."

"Thank you," replied Monique.

"I love when girls ride bikes," Felicia said.

"Yeah, we ain't got to be on the back of them all the time," Saree added.

"I love dis neighborhood. You think they got some apartments for rent around here?" Teresa asked.

"Is that one of y'all cars up front?" Felicia asked. "Well, where can I get some seat covers like that?"

"They're exclusive," Ronisa told her. "But remind me to give you this business card before y'all leave, okay?"

# Chapter 28

I was drunk, talking shit and having fun. And now I'm walking to the bathroom and Sofia was coming out. I stepped one way and she stepped that way with me. And then I stepped to the other side and she stepped to that side too. She looked me in the eyes, close as fuck.

"Damn. Why is the good ones always taken?" she said. She rubbed my stomach and slid her hand toward my johnson, surprising the shit out of me. Yeah, I wasn't expecting that; then she kissed me.

"Oh, sorry!" Monique said. She had seen us while she was going to the bathroom. Damn. If she did see something, I guarantee that Felicia's going to hear about this.

"She did what?! Uh-uh. Hell naw!" yelled Felicia.

Damn! That little bitch had to say something. And before I knew it, they had already pulled off their chains and kicked off their sandals. Felicia handed Monique the keys and told her to put their stuff in the car. "Here, Mo-Mo, put this stuff up."

"I knew that I came over here for a good reason," Felicia said. "Bitch is you fucking crazy? My cuz said that you kissed my dude," Felicia screamed.

"Girl, calm down. I don't think that she'd kiss yo dude, honey," Lisa said.

"I seen her. Clear as day," Monique said. She was already back from the car and was taking her earrings out.

"Well, she shouldn't have done that," Ronisa said.

"Y'all, please take that outside. Please don't fight in here," Lisa said.

Sofia came out the cut. "Yeah, bitch! I kissed him and what? I take what I want. What? You think I'm some pussyclot girl?"

"Black, grab Saree," I said.

I grabbed Felicia and told Antonio to get his sister.

I was still stunned on how this night just flipped to a nightmare out of nowhere. Then a Patron bottle hit Felicia on the shoulder. We both ducked, and then I tried to grab her, but she slipped through my hands and they all rushed at Sofia. Monique ran up and immediately started swinging at Sofia and the twins.

"Somebody grab them, please," Lisa said.

"Get the fuck off me," Felicia said. And that's when Lisa started flipping.

"Now I asked you little bitches nicely. I told you motherfuckas not to fight in my house," *Pow! Pow! Pow!*

Lisa shot her .38 in the air.

"I barely got nothing now," Lisa said. "And y'all trying to tear up what little shit that I got."

Then my phone started ringing in the middle of all the commotion. I couldn't miss any business so I answered it.

"Hello? Auntie?" I was in the hallway now, hitting the steps, trying to get away from any stray bullets. "Auntie, I'ma call you right back. It's some crazy shit going on right now." Lisa and Ronisa were flipping out.

I ended the call just when I heard Lisa shout, "Get out, you little dumb ass hoodlums and hoes. That's why I don't like bitches now." She was still gripping her gun, ready to bust again. Monique hit the stairs after me, getting the last words in.

"Shut the fuck up, you old ass bitch!"

Lisa was staggering drunk and started popping again when we hit the door. Then we all shot out the door in a reckless line.

"And don't comeback you little dirty ass heifers," Ronisa said.

Lisa was buzzing like a mug. And a nigga damn near got hit. If she hadn't been as drunk as she was then somebody would have got it.

Everybody followed Black and Saree, running behind them to the back of the building that was two apartments down from Lisa's. We stopped running when we thought we were clear. Heavy breathing, hands on our knees, hunched over. Running wasn't for us.

"Damn, them old bitches is crazy."

I was holding Felicia's hand; then she started to throw up from the rum and the liquor.

"Uueeegh! Euuhhh!"

"Damn, Bay. You alright?" I said.

"Ta, shut up. I'm still mad at you," Felicia said, with slob still around her mouth from calling Earl.

The other girls were coughing and throwing up too. See, that's the difference between bar drinking and free hand drinking out of Styrofoam cups. Everybody was skunky drunk.

"I wasn't going to do any more fighting," Felicia said.

"Shit, mon," Antonio said, looking upset.

"What's wrong?" I said.

"How is we supposed to get our bikes, mon? That crazy woman might still be shooting," Antonio said.

"Man, y'all gone have to wait until the rollers leave," I said.

Black started laughing. "What the fuck is everybody tripping on? That was some funny shit" he finally said after he finished laughing. "Man, Felicia and Saree, this ain't even about to jump off. We do business with them," Black said.

"Well, business don't consist of that hoe pushing up on my girl's man," Saree said.

"My sister don't drink that often. I apologize for her. She had to be a little too drunk," Antonio said.

"Shut the fuck up!" Monique said, out of nowhere.

"Eh, mon! Watch yo bloodclot mouth," Antonio said. I could tell by his clenched jaw that he was catching himself from doing what he really wanted to do, which was slap Monique for keeping up the bullshit.

"Man, Monique, chill out," I said. "Look I don't know what went down but check, we about this feddy, right? Tonio you still gonna bubble at the college and me and Black is gone stay on this grind, so we need to squash the bullshit, right?" I said.

"Man, and I'ma keep it real... I think they're a little too drunk to be riding and driving," Black said.

"Look, I'ma drop y'all off downtown to the telly and we'll get the bikes first thing in the morning," I said.

"Uhuhh! That whore is not riding with us."

"Man, Felicia, chill. This night is over. Black follow me down here to drop them off downtown. Y'all ride with him," I said.

"Eh, how do we know that nobody's gonna steal our bikes?" said Antonio.

"Y'all should be cool, but this night is over," I said. I was getting fed up with the whole situation.

"Well, I'm riding with Black if she's gonna be in the car," Felicia said, pointing to Sofia.

"Hell naw! I already know, Ma. That's a fight waiting to happen," I said.

We jumped in the whips and I followed Black downtown. Sofia and her family was riding with me and she looked geeked up and somewhat out of her character, but everybody got their fucked up days. This was the girls time over doing it. Shiit, I done spazzed out so many times before that I had to forgive them anyway. My whole thing was that if it wasn't for Sofia sliding me that receipt that night, we would have still been getting questioned in the city jail right now. Therefore, she was my nigga for life for that. That shit that she did in the house just surprised me, but it didn't thrill me, 'cause when I say I'm on my grind, then I mean I'm on my grind.

*You have an incoming call from Peaches.*

"Hello. What's up, Peaches?"

"Nothing, Ta. But tell me how did I hook you up with friends and now she's calling me talking about y'all is disrespectful and she don't care how much money y'all is giving her, and she don't want y'all back over there and she said come and get them goddamn motorcycles up out of her yard," Peaches said all in one breath.

"Tell her we'll come get them tomorrow," I said.

"Okay. I'll let her know. But Ta, what did y'all do?" asked Peaches.

"Nothing."

"Naw. Y'all did something," Peaches said.

"Okay, the girls started arguing. A bottle got thrown, and that's it," I said, exhaling from frustration. "Then yo friends started firing like crazy," I added.

"Haa! Haahaaha!'" Peaches just busted out laughing.

"What's so funny?"

"That girl is still crazy. Y'all must have been fighting in her house. She don't go for that shit. I'll tell her that you're coming to get them bikes tomorrow. Early, right?" Peaches asked.

"Yeah, but Peaches, tell her I'm sorry, alright?" I said, thinking mainly about my grind.

"Okay, but where is you at? 'Cause I'm trying to come meet you real fast. I'm about to leave my job," Peaches said.

"You work at the hospital, right? Well, if you're coming, come right now and meet me at the Hilton 'cause I'm headed there now. I'ma be there in about ten minutes. It shouldn't take you longer than that to get down there from where you are. And be there, Babe, because this night is over," I said.

Peaches repeated after me. "Over." she said.

"Yep. Over," I assured her.

I dropped Tonio and the girls off. Then I seen Peaches parked in a peach colored Mustang. I swear she stayed on some fly shit."

She rung me just as I pulled up. "Hello, yeah. I see you." I got in the car.

"What's up, Ma? What was you trying to do?"

"Here's a hundred dollars. Let me get a quake," Peaches said. She looked in her car mirror. Checking her face.

"Damn girl, you is killing. Here. Fuck it," I said.

"Now, tell me what happened," Peaches said.

She was moving so fast. She broke down the weed on a CD case, and licked and split the blunt quick. Then she blazed before I even got two words out.

"Damn, you acted like you needed that," I said.

"Yeah, I did, Ta. It's my job," Peaches said.

"Your job?"

"Yeah, it's cool, but this patient that I got been stressing me out lately. I mean, you know I'm hood too, but this dude just be on some straight bullshit all day. He ain't got no manners and his broke ass stay trying to holla at me. You might know him?" Peaches said. "His name is__

*Call from* . . . "Hold up," I said, answering the call. "Hello."

"Yeah, man, what's up?"

"Yeah, man, we need to get these girls to the house," Black said, sounding as if his patience was running thin also.

"Alright, Ma," I said to Peaches. I had to pull out. "I'ma holla at your later. And tell your friends that I said I'm sorry and can we still keep the grind going."

"Okay bohhy, but you gone have to keep yo girls in check."

"You right, Babe," I said. "I'll get with you later."

Yeah and if you know Felicia, she'll probably check herself. I probably a be salty too if a nigga kissed my boo.

I rode over to Black's and swooped up Felicia. I put her in the car and slid into the driver's side. I looked over at her. My baby was on the passenger's side *wasted*. I shook my head. This is a night that I wish I could just pull straight up in the driveway and walk straight in the house. But I'm in the game, and in this lifestyle I can never do that. Especially with my boo in the car. A nigga be too over protective. So I circled the strip twice, then backed up into the driveway.

"Come on, Boo," I said.

"Huh!" Felicia said. I could tell that she was still out of it.

Damn. I carried her in the house and put her in the bed. I took off her sandals and lied beside her and went to sleep.

## Chapter 29

*Call from Black.*

"Hello, man. What's up, my dude? It's 1pm. What? You gone sleep all day?" Black asked.

"Naw."

"Shiit, last night was hectic and I ain't even get a chance to count the money," he said.

"Okay," I said, shaking my head. "Yeah, I'm up. We supposed to hook up with Will. Hold on a minute, Bliz," I said.

"Hello." I answered the phone.

"Ta, this is Sofia. Antonio told me what happened last night. I'm sorry. I mean, so sorry, Ta. Is your girl around so I can apologize?" Sofia said.

"That's alright, Ma. She understands."

"Ta, we got to go and get our bikes."

"Damn, that's right. I'ma call Lisa and let her know that y'all coming to get them," I said.

"Ta, we don't have any way to get there. Plus that woman's crazy. I need you to come with us, alright?" Sofia said.

"Damn, alright," I said. "I'll be there in a minute. Be ready, alright?"

"Okay," she said and hung up the phone.

I clicked back over and told Black the change in plans. Then I called Will to make sure that we could still get them whips.

"Hello," I said. "I was just making sure we was still on this morning."

"Yeah, I'll be home in an hour, Youngsta. Thanks for keeping the car for me, too," Will said.

"Eh, Will? How much would it cost for me to get two of these whips?"

"Well, let me call Mike at the dealership, and I'll let him know that you're a close buddy. Then we'll go from there," Will said.

"Alright, you got it. Holla in a minute," I said.

I glanced out the rearview mirror. *Why do this motherfucka look like he's following me?* I thought to myself. I pulled up to the telly and called Sofia.

"Hello, this is Sofia."

"Yeah, what's going on," I said.

"Yeah, Ta we're coming down right now."

They came out the door. Sofia looked revived and fresh, and the twins did also.

"Okay, you good today, right?" I said, when they got in the car.

"You mean sober, right?" Sofia said.

"You said it, not me," I said, always keeping focus on the road.

"Ta, I'm really sorry about last night, and we probably won't come back to Cleveland for a while. So Tonio asked me to ask you if he could get another quarter pound?" Sofia said.

"Yeah Ma. Go in that bag for me and give him them couple of bags," I said. "So, Sofia, do you really think I'm cute?" I was kind of fishing and kinda curious.

"No silly. I told you that I was drunk. And I don't drink that often. I was what y'all say, out of my hook up."

"Yeah?" I asked. My tone was sarcastic. "Cause personally, I thought you were maintaining."

"Shut up, Ta. Well anyway I'm sorry, okay?"

"Believe me, I'm from Cleveland, and things like that happens all the time. Hold up. Let me make this call," I said.

"Hello Lisa," I said, when she picked up the phone. "Did you talk to Peaches?"

"Yeah, I talked to her."

"So did she tell you that I said I'm sorry," I said.

"You sorry, huh? Mister Charm Tashawn. Come and get those bikes out my yard, boy," Lisa said.

"I'll be there in a few minutes. What about what we been on? Can we still KIM?" I asked.

"KIM? Boy, speak English. I don't understand what you're talking about. What the hell is KIM?"

"Keep it moving," I said.

"Oh. Ta, I don't know about that yet. You're gonna have to call me later and I'll let you know. But if I do, you better not bring them little bitches around here," Lisa said.

I pulled up to Lisa's house and asked if they we're cool.

Sofia said, "Yeah." But to me, they looked like they were kinda crunched up.

"Ta, can I call you?" Sofia asked.

"Yeah. Call me and let me know that y'all made it back alright," I said.

"Mon, you sure that woman not gonna trip, right?" Tonio said. "Alright, then make sure you get it."

"Bet," I said. They got the bikes, I gave him dap and left.

I went to the house and changed clothes and switched up on the wheels, and grabbed some paper out the stash. This shit right here is gonna hurt. "Hello." I answered the phone.

"Yeah, this is Will right here. Yeah, Youngsta, what's going on?"

"What's up, Will?"

"I'm just letting you know that I'm home, man," Will said.

"Okay. I'll be there in a minute," I said.

"Oh yeah. I called about the vehicle and Mike said that he'll give you an identical model of mine's. Mine's is going for the same."

"What you mean, 'yours?'"

"Yeah. I'ma sell mine to you. And who's the other one for?" Will asked.

"My buddy," I replied.

"Well, you know that's pretty much a deal. These old schools got everything new in them under the hood. As you can see, everything is chrome and not painted. Real stuff," Will said. "Mike had said that he could easily charge you fifty for both of them – twenty-five 'piece."

"Damn. Alright. Then where do you want to meet?"

"We'll meet on the west side at Mike's Oldsmobile in about thirty minutes," Will said.

"Oh, yeah__What's up with Galena? Is she alright?" I asked.

"What you mean?" Will asked.

"I mean-is she cool? Remember you said that she suffered from a heat stroke. I prayed for her one night," I said.

"Oh yeah? Yeah, she's fine, Ta. Thanks for being so concerned, too," Will said. "Alright. Thirty minutes."

"Yep, thirty minutes it is then."

I called Black. "This shit's fucked up," I said.

"What, man?" Black asked.

"Man, you can't even imagine how fucked up this shit is."

"Man, what Ta? Spit it out."

"Alright, man. It's fucked up that we gone be riding old school back-to-back," I said.

"Oh yeah?" Black said.

"Hell yeah, Dawg. I'm that nigga, right?"

"Yeah, you that nigga," Black said. "And you're my nigga for life."

"Partner for life," I said, correcting Black.

"Whatever, man. I'm just glad that you put that move down," Black said.

"Yeah, but it's gone run us about forty racks. Like twenty apiece."

"Shiit," Black said.

"Man, we spend this forty, I'ma have to get back," I said. "Shiit, I'm taking all sales 'cause now I'm pushing myself further away from that goal. We've been jacking off money all this week, so you know what it is. Pirating. Straight Pirating. Pirating on water, searching for treasures."

"Let's do it. As long as we stay on our grind, then we can still reach that number that we're shooting for," Black said.

"Man, grab some squares. Where you at? I'm on my way to come get you."

"I'm at Saree's house," he said.

"Alright. I'll be there in a second."

"One."

"One." I hung up.

"Hello. Yeah, this is Will. Remember you asked me to give you something. Well, I got it."

"You said that you got something? Well, you better not be pulling my coat, William," a voice on the other side of the phone line said.

"Naw, man, believe me. This is real shit," Will said.

"Look here, buddy. If you don't have all the cash, then fuck off. My daughter's tuition is due. I gotta pay two house notes and sometimes I just like to have some extra cash just for the fuck of it. Maybe I want a blowjob. Maybe I want a T-bone steak or whatever. So therefore, I can't do it, so good-bye," Mike said, and snapped his flip phone shut without hearing what else Will had to say.

# Chapter 30

I picked up Black, then jumped straight on the freeway.

"Yeah, put that shit in the air, man. We can't take no more days off. Ya hear me?" I said.

We made it to the west side in twenty-five minutes. Five minutes early. Will was already there. "What's up, Will?" I asked.

"Ta, what's up?" Will said. He gave me a hand clap and a hug at the same time.

Will was in beige linen and had a few gold rings. He always looked playerish.

"Eh, who's the gentleman right here?" Will asked.

"This is my partner, Black. Black, Will. Will, Black."

"What's going on, Will?" Black asked. He extended his hand, giving Will an unusual handshake.

"Okay fellows, let me introduce you to my good friend, Mike. Mike, this is Ta. And this is Black. A couple of fine young men," Will said.

"Now what's up, guys? What can I do for you?" Mike asked, staring at us.

"Yeah, man, we need those two old schools," I said.

"Well, those what you're talking about is some newly rebuilt engines. Expensive pieces of equipment, man. And let me tell you, I charge $25,000 apiece for them. But since you guys are Will's people, then I might take something off," Mike explained. "Now you guys can give me $45,000 with a car note," he said. I couldn't tell if he was bluffing or not.

"Look, man. We got forty right now, so what's up? You gone shoot or dribble? What the fuck is you gone do, Bob or Mike or whatever your name is?" I said.

"The name is Mike, kid. And do you guys even got license? Because if not then__

"Forty," I said, cutting him off. "Eh Black, hand me that bag." Once I got it, I threw it over to Mike.

"Do we need to count?" I asked with a confident smile on my face.

"Nope," Mike answered. He seemed to choke on his words.

"Well, slide us them keys," I said. He could see in my face I meant business.

"You guys said this is forty, right?" He looked at us, then over at Will and smiled. "Man, Will, I don't know where you got these guys from, but I like them," Mike said, wiping the sweat off his forehead.

A nigga threw that $40,000 like it was nothing. But me and Black both knew that it hurt. Especially when we was chasing that goal. Fuck it. We'll re-up. Plus, the phones been jumping, so everything should pan out.

"Ta, I need you to come right here for a second," Will said. "I need to cop a pound real fast."

"Right here? You sure you ain't trying to wait until I come pick up my car from yo house?" I asked.

I figured that he had to sell some weed to Mike or something real quick. You know, that's probably why he stayed out of trouble, 'cause he kept his clientele like that. But still Will was discreet, so discreet that Will wasn't the type that a switch up, and I personally couldn't see him doing business here. But fuck it, 'cause I need to get back anyway from just spending that cash on them whips.

"Five thousand five hundred, Will."

"Okay, here you go, Ta. And call me whenever you're coming to pick up your ride. I can come get you if you want, 'cause remember, I still don't want anybody else around the house. Cool?" Will said.

"Yeah, that's cool." I agreed.

"But, I'm sure that you and Black want to show off your new rides right now. Or like y'all younstas say, I'm sure y'all ready to go stunt out," Will said.

"You already know," I said, giving Will dap, plus the hug to go along with it. "But the truth is that we ain't really got much time to stunt, floss, show out, cap, or show everybody that we came down. None of that shit right now, so you can call me, Will, if you need something else 'cause that's all that we doing right now." We too outta there, doe. Keys, titles, back-to-back.

We left the car we came in and slid out of there. Man, a nigga was feeling eighteen again. But this was just an average toy right now, but in about three weeks we rimming these puppies up.

I was sliding through my old hood, then trailing Black while he was sliding through his old hood, turning up 131st Street and just riding. I turned down my uncle's street off the First, where my grandma used to live at. It always felt like home; every time I came on this street.

I pulled up and my little cousins was in the front yard playing.

"Ta, what's up? Let me get five dollars."

"Here go ten...and ten and ten." I passed out the money. "Now y'all get what y'all want," I said.

"Man, Ta, where did you get that Hot Wheels car from?"

"These is old schools," I said.

"That's fly shit," Lil' Dre said.

"What's up, Black? You a sucka," Lil' Red said.

"What? Come here, lil chump," Black said, playing with the youngstas. He looked at me. "Man, I'm tripping on how they be talking fly already."

"Nigga, we box. Plus, we know karate and we ain't no chumps," Lil' Dre said.

"Raphael, where's Unc at?"

"He's in the house. You want me to go get him for you?" Raphael, the youngest out the three, asked.

"Naw, I'll get him. Anyway I thought y'all was going to the store."

"Man, we wanna ride in the Hot Wheels car," Raphael said.

"Man, quit calling it that. It's an old school, Raphael," Lil' Dre said.

"That's right. An old school Cutlass," I said.

"And look, the store is right there." I pointed down the street to the corner. "So y'all can walk. I'll come and get y'all later on this week," I said.

Black was on the phone with his finger up, like 'hold up.' Then he said, "I'll take them to the store real quick."

"Yaaay!" all three of the boys said. They were excited about riding in the new car.

"Man, y'all talking 'bout '*yaaay*,' sounding like some little girls," I said. I liked to pick with them.

"Shut up, punk," Lil' Red said.

"Yeah, shut up," they all said together.

"Ahhh! I was just playing, lil niggas." I looked at Black. "Eh, Black be careful with them. You know they some little hoodlums."

"I can handle them. I got a few little brothers of my own," Black said.

"Hey, Auntie Debra." I walked into the house.

"Eh, close that goddamn door," Auntie Debra yelled.

"Damn, Auntie. That's how I get treated when I come around?"

"Ta!" She looked up from the flat screen. "Ta, I thought you was them bad ass boys. G Wow. I ain't seen you in a minute."

Auntie Debra's mood changed from bad to good soon as she noticed me. "Keith. Keith," she repeated a little louder. "Look what the wind blew in. Yo nephew's here."

"Auntie, Black took the kids to the corner store."

"Yo friend, Black? How has he been doing? He was such a well-mannered boy. Yeah, is he alright?" Auntie asked.

"Yeah. He doing good."

"Good. And that's fine with me that he took them, but tell him just don't press no charges against me, 'cause they gone drive that man crazy. Them boys are bad," said Auntie, shaking her head.

"They ain't bad; they're just young," Uncle Keith said as he walked into the room.

"Okay, if you say so," Auntie Debra said as she disappeared to the kitchen.

"So Unc, what's been up?"

"Nothing much. How have you been doing, nephew?"

"I've been alright," I said. I handed him a sac. "Try this out on GP, Unc. Plus, I want you to check out my new wheels," I said.

"Oh yeah? Come on. I want to see this."

"Whoaa Ta! Now that's what I'm talking bout." We had stepped outside and was standing on the porch. "That's nice right there. Real nice," Uncle Keith said, getting taken off guard a bit from how nice the Cutty was.

"Yeah? You think so?" I asked.

"Hell yeah, boy. That's a work of art right there."

"Well, you can use it anytime you want," I said. I gave Unc a hand clap with a hug.

"Alright now. I might take you up on that one."

He stepped off the porch and walked around the car, smiling the whole time. "Man, where did you get this beauty from?"

"My dude, Ole Will, plugged me in with this guy, Mike. He got a dealership, and me and Black both copped one for a real nice price. But now I need to get some of that cash that I spent back, understand me?" I asked.

Unc nodded his head and said, "Yes sir. I feel you all the way."

"You said Ole Will, right? I'm trying to figure out why that names sounds so familiar," Uncle Keith said, with a puzzled type of face, like he was thinking really hard.

"Yeah, he said that he used to stay around here. Shiit on the next street over, actually."

Uncle Keith put his finger on his forehead and thought. "The only Will I knew should be still doing time right now for accessory to murder." I looked at him with a surprised look on my face.

"Yeah, he was supposed to go on an easy move with this nigga named Dean. The move didn't go as smooth as it was planned so Dean ended up pulling the trigger and got twenty-five to life."

"And damn, now that I think about it, I don't know what happened to Will." He shook his head. "It probably ain't the same dude anyway." He smiled at me. "What's up, doe, nephew? Do you want something to drink? I can stir you up a Long Island Iced Tea, real quick," Uncle Keith said. He held open the screen door and I followed him in.

"Naw, I would Unc, but I'm back on my all day grind so I'm trying to keep my head clear," I said.

"Hold up, let me call Pete and check on something real quick." My uncle picked up his cell phone and made a call.

"Pete, what's going on with ya? I ain't trying to hear that man. Kill yo'self," said Unc, sharing a loud laugh over the phone. "Yeah my nephew's over here and believe me when I say that he got some steam. Send him around? Alright, you got it. Hahahaha. It's always a plus to have an old buddy," said Uncle Keith, as he was hanging the phone up.

"He said he wants you to come around there, Ta. Most likely he'll spend two hundred," Unc said. "You remember where he stay right?"

"Yeah on 136th; make a right on the dead end street."

"What's going on, Unc Keith?" Black walked in.

"Oh, that's Black," I said.

"What' up young'un? How the hell are you?" Uncle Keith said.

Black had come in with the boys. They had boxes of burgers and fries and brown bags that was full of candy, pops and Debbie snacks.

We headed out and got in our cars. My aunt and uncle walked us to the door. Auntie was in the screen door waving.

"Nice cars," she said, complimenting me and Black. One was cool, but they we're on a different level seeing both of them together.

"Thanks, Ms. Debra. It ain't really nothing, doe," Black said.

"Okay. I'll see y'all later, but you boys be careful alright?"

# Chapter 31

You know we went straight back to the grind.

"Follow me to the gas station," I said to Black.

We rolled up in the Marathon with our sound up loud. Boppers around staring 'cause we was killing everything in there, even without the rims. Boppers were walking up trying to holla off rip. One nigga walked up mean mugging while Black was pumping his gas. He looked me up and down, walked past my car, then walked past Black's car, and then flew spit. A glob landed right on Black's whip.

"Shiit, ain't no wind blowing," Black said, looking dude up and down. "Man, what the fuck? You just spit on my shit!" Black blew up. "I know you ain't just spit on my shit!"

"Naw, my dude. You must have drove into it," said dude that spit, snickering like he found it funny.

"Nigga, my fucking car is parked!" yelled Black.

I immediately went and grabbed the hammer, but before I did, Black started instantly dogging dude with his hands. He hit the nigga with everything.

I jumped right in to instigate. I told him to throw. "Yeah, bohhy. Left jab. Left jab. Right over. Yeah one more time, Black," I said, coaching Black on in the fight.

He hit him one more time then he started picking his punches, embarrassing the fuck out of dude in front of all the broads that were up there. Now they start waving their hands down at dude and calling him a punk.

"What happened? Why is they fighting?" one girl in the crowd asked.

"Giiirl__that nigga that's getting his ass beat was hating and spit on that one's car," explained one of the bopper girls.

I saw a nigga out the corner of my eye. *'This nigga keeps getting closer and closer,'* I thought to myself. "Hey," I spoke up. "My nigga, it's one-on-one. Respect that," I said.

Dude tried to grab Black, but he ducked and weaved and hit the nigga with two flush punches straight down the middle. Then he pulled dude's shirt over his head and wiped the spit off his car with it. Then the dude I had my eye on tried to run up on Black, so I stepped in and pivoted and caught his boy with a clean shot.

I'm like, "Get the fuck away from my nigga, bitch! I told you this was one on one."

*"Whaaaaam!"* My head jerked back. "Man, did this nigga just hit me with a brick?" I felt it. I was still standing, staggering, doe. Then I picked up a pipe and *"Flap! Flap! Flap! Flap!"* I just got to busing at niggas and people started scattering everywhere. I took one step towards the whip and passed out.

I woke up on the passenger's side of my own car on the next street over. One of the chicks from the gas station was sitting in the driver's seat with an ice pack on my head. Black opened up the door, got in the back seat, and gave her fifty dollars for driving me around there while he tailed them in his car.

"No thanks," said the bopper, and gave Black back the money. "Uhh uh, Boo," she said. "Them niggas is always starting some shit."

"Shiit, doe; here go a sack at least," said Black.

"Is you alright?" asked the bopper, rubbing on the side of my head. I had woke up smiling. "You must be from the Wild Wild West," said girly.

"Man, get yo punk ass up." Black said, punching my arm. "You gone let that nigga hit you with a brick?" he said, playing around. "But glad to see you is cool."

"Damn. A nigga hit me with a brick?" I said, trying to shake it off, my vision still slightly impaired. "Then what did I do?" I said.

"What did you do? Yo crazy ass shot up the whole lot," Black said.

"Damn. Where's my hammer at?" I asked, reaching for my hip, realizing that it was missing.

"Man, chill. I got it right here. And do you think you need to go to the hospital?"

"Naw, I'm cool. And thank you too, young lady," I said.

"No problem," she said. "You just owe me a ride in this car."

"Shiit, that's cool with me," I said. "Go head and put the number in my phone, and I'ma lock you in. Bet?"

"Okay, bet," she said. She smiled to let me know that I really had made her day.

I tried to smile at her, but the whole side of my face was still hurting. I had a knot on my head and maybe a minor concussion. But I couldn't afford to sit off in the hospital all day. Fuck that. I gots to make some chips.

"Eh, try and holler at Lisa, Black. Think she still fucks with you?" I asked.

"Hello, can I speak to Lisa?" Black put the phone on speaker.

"This is her. Who is this?"

"Hey Lisa, this Black. What's up with you, Ma?" Is everything back yet?" Black asked.

"Black, did Ta tell you to call? Well, you tell him that I'll call y'all when I'm ready," she yelled and then hung up the phone.

"Hello? Damn!" She hung up. Man!" Black said, sounding frustrated. "Man, she's salty," he added, shaking his head. "Damn, this shit's crazy. Can't go to Ronisa's house. Them niggas from the Bricks is probably just waiting in the cut, ready to blame a nigga."

Man, I had got $125,000, and Black said he had racked up 'bout $100,000. Man, it's slow out here, and a nigga trying to get that $20,000 back.

Luther called back like, "What's up, bohhy? Did you drop them prices, yet?"

For some reason a paranoid feeling came over me like six five was on the line with us so I hung up.

The phone rang again. "Hello. Yeah man, what's up?" I said, sounding aggravated.

"Yeah, man, why you hang up on me?"

"'Cause you light weight talking crazy, bohhy," I said. "Eh Luth, what is you trying to do? Matter-of-fact, I'ma just blow down on you," I said. I was right down the street from him anyway. I could see him as we pulled up.

"Let me get a – Damn! I see y'all came down," Luth said, admiring the cars together. "Man, I'm trying to come down old school, too," Luth added.

"Alright then, Luth. I'm gone put you together this time. Give me forty-five hundred for the whole P," I said.

"Yeah, that's what I'm talking 'bout," Luth said, slapping me some dap from being amped up about receiving a sweet price again.

"And if you want, I'll even give you a spot to work out of," I offered.

"A spot? Naw. I'm cool on that, Ta. I got my own clientele, but if you want me to break bread, I'm with that."

"Naw, my nigga just handle yo' business, and don't be complaining about the prices."

"Whatever," Luth said. "Just keep it plain and don't be going up and down on that see-saw shit."

"I got you. Bet. And I'ma try to get them lower than that for you," I said.

"Bet!" said Luth. "Man, what the fuck happened to yo' dome?" Luther examined my face, looking at it up and down.

"Long story," I replied, thinking about that brick going upside my head.

"Alright, but let me know if somebody's fucking with you," Luth said, joking with me like I needed a bodyguard.

"Man, what was yo' fat ass gone do anyway, Luth?"

Luth put his arm up like he was making a muscle and said, "I's all muscle under here, bohhy."

So I tapped the gas pedal. *Vroom vroom.* "And this is all muscle under this hood, nigga."

"That's cool. I'ma get one of them bitches next. I'm out, doe, Ta. But just for the record, one of my little chicks told me that she seen you get hit with a brick earlier. And she said that you and that crazy ass nigga, right there, was out there shooting, too. Man, *you never know* who might of got yo' plates, fool. What happened to keeping it plain, and getting money man, you know? It's hard to get dough when drama's around," Luth said. He put his hand through the window and placed it on my shoulder. He had a serious look on his face.

"Damn, you right, man. Good looking, Luth. That shit was real. Call me when you ready, doe, my nigga. Peace."

Sometimes in life you start feeling like…, you start feeling like everything in the world revolves around you. Whenever you got a feeling like that, then you either step up to the plate as a leader or you fall all the way back. But see, I was kinda lingering around on some Magic Johnson shit, always passing the buck. I knew that I was that nigga but I kept downplaying it; thinking that one day I might escape this shit for some reason. I think everybody knew how deep in the game I was except for me.

"Hello."

"Nigga, I'm gone body yo' bitch ass when I see you, lame."

"Man, quit calling my phone, Snitch!" I yelled into the phone, not knowing who the stalking voice on the phone was.

In fact, now that I think about it, I can read a sign, 'cause these niggas wants to kill me. So I'ma end up having to kill them, and either way it go, ain't no money getting made in that situation.

"Hello. What's up, Bay? Do you still gotta hangover?"

"Yeah. Ta, can you bring me some aspirin when you come back?" asked Felicia.

"Yeah Ma, but check this out. You start school in two months, right? Yeah well, Boo, I think that we should go out there for a few years and get established. Yeah, and I might wanna sign up for community college and try to get a business degree," I said.

"Yeah, Bay, that's a good idea. So you just want to up and leave in two months?" Felicia asked.

"Naw, Bay. I'm talking one or two days."

"What about our responsibilities, Ta?"

"Well, I'll probably rent out the spot," I said.

"And my father will most likely be alright with his business," Felicia added.

"I already got a few dollars. Just let me make a couple of more moves and we should be alright," I said.

"Okay, Ta. But just come home soon, alright?"

"Alright."

I went and parked the whip and rolled shotgun in Black's old school.

"Hello. What's up, girl?" I said.

"I said that I'll call *you*!" Lisa said, hanging up on me again.

"Man, Lisa's tripping," I said, as I sat back in the seat, trying to figure out another plan.

"Man, fuck that bitch. Yeah, fuck jocking that bitch all day," Black said. "Man, put something in the air," he said.

"Man, you know that I'm thinking 'bout bouncing, right?" I said, exhaling smoke.

"Bouncing? What about our goal we set?" Black asked, with a confused look on his face. He shook his head like he was disappointed.

"Shiit, it can still be reached, but this bitch is starting to get too hot. I suggest that you make a move too, ya dig," I said.

"Make a move where? I mean, where do I gots to go?" Black said.

I could see that my nigga was on it too, but just didn't know where to go. And for some reason I felt like I would've been leaving a mess, and I just couldn't leave him like that. Plus, this nigga was something like a little brother to me, you know? More than a partner.

"Eh, why don't you and Saree come with us?" I said.

"Naw, man. I ain't trying to intrude on 'y'all's dreams."

"This ain't no dream, Black. This is a power move and a business plan. And since we're business partners, I think that you should make that move with me."

"Man, I don't know, Ta. I don't know how Saree would feel about this. And what about our B.Ms?" Black continued.

Then I cut him off saying, "Man, we ain't gone be no good for them if we're locked up, or dead for that matter. You feel me? Look, we'll send for them. Man, start making good decisions, Bleed. Quit being clueless. We're the men. We'll put them in some fly shit and move them into some nice apartments. Shiiit. I ain't hustling for nothing. I don't know about you. Yeah, what about you?" I turned and looked at him. "Say it with me," I said. "I ain't hustling for nothing. I ain't hustling for nothing," Black and I said together.

"Man, you silly as fuck," Black said. Then he finally broke down. "Yeah let's roll." He gave me some dap like he was all the way with it.

# Chapter 32

"So let's roll 'cause we gots to get back for them whips," I said.

"So how much profit did we make today?" I asked.

"Like $5,700," Black said. "Maybe a little less."

"Damn! Man, Lisa's on some bullshit and I needs to get back," I said, sounding like a broken record from only one thing being on my mind.

"So we gone be neighbors like Fred and Barney, huh?" Black said.

"Ahhhh! You silly for that one," I said.

I usually don't answer the other phone, and really don't answer private calls, but was so thirsty that I wasn't even thinking.

"Hello. Yeah, call back and let your number show," I said.

*Call from 7-9-9.* "Yeah. Hello," I answered.

"Yeah, what's up my dude," said the stranger's voice.

"Yo, dude, who the fuck is you, my dude?" I said, souring, slightly cautious.

"This is Eli, my nigga," said the caller.

"Eli, huh?"

"Yeah, Eli. You probably don't remember, doe, 'cause it don't seem like you want to fuck with a real nigga."

"Yeah, I do, but it's been kinda slow," I said.

Black was waving his hand and whispered, "Don't hang up, Ta. See what that nigga want. I'm trying to get back some of them ends we spent."

"Man, hold up." I put the phone down to holla at Black for a second.

"Shiit, I don't really fuck with this cat," I said.

"My nigga, every dollar counts right now. Especially if we planning on dipping out of town," Black said.

I shook my head knowing that I was going against my gut feeling. *Fuck it. We do need this money,* I thought.

"Yeah, hello. What was you trying to do?"

"Like 2 P's"

"Yeah, that's cool but you know that's gone hit you for $12 thousand," I said.

"Oh, that's sweet right now. Where you trying to meet up at?" Eli asked.

"Meet me at Walmart on the Westside."

"Bet. I'll be there in fifteen minutes," Eli said.

"Yeah, man, I don't really feel this nigga," I said, looking over at Black. "It's just something about this nigga that makes me not trust him."

"I know, but let's hit his corny ass for these 2 P's and then this day won't be so bad," Black said, talking with one hand on the steering wheel, explaining on how you play some cats for what they're worth.

We pulled up in Walmart and the lot was full.

"Hello, I'm in the back of the parking lot. What is you sliding in?" Eli asked.

"I'm in an old school Cutty."

"What is y'all driving?" I asked.

"I'm in a navy colored Monte Carlo. One of the newer ones," Eli explained.

"Oh, alright, I see you. Let's make this quick," I said. "Black, hand me those two."

"Yo. here go the money," Eli said

"Hold up. Count it out, Black."

Black whipped through that shit like a money machine.

"It's all there."

"Alright. Here you go," I said, handing Eli the trees.

I let Eli sit in the front seat so I could watch him from the blindside and Black had his side view. Everything weighed up right, so he nodded to his big nigga like everything was good.

Eli got out, then I got out and was about to hop in the front seat, but before that I gave the nigga some dap.

I got in the car and he was like, "*Ta*, I'ma hit you as soon as I get rid of these."

'Hold up,' I thought. 'Back track.'

"*My nigga, they call me Eli. Who to ask for when I call, my nigga?*"

"*Yeah, ask for P.Air P.Air P.Air.*"

"Black watch out!" I said, reaching for my hammer. *Blaablhbalah.*

I upped as soon as I heard him call my name.

*Blaca Blaca Blaca Blaca.*

Black was busting too, emptying out his whole clip, and then started reloading.

"Damn, Black! Roll out," I said while ducking down in the seat, busting my hammer.

But Black wasn't moving. Damn my nigga looking fucked up over there. I seen Eli hit the ground.

"Black! Hold up my nigga."

My nigga was over there leaking, so I grabbed the wheel and peeled out. That nigga was busing some automatic shit at us. I smacked like three cars driving from the passenger's side. "Dawg, you hit." I hit a couple side streets, pulled up and ran up on a curve, smacked a tree, but had enough time to get this nigga to the passenger's side.

"Dawg, *you are hit*, my Nigga. I'ma get you to the hospital." I tossed the hammers in a gutter. "Alright, we almost there."

I called 911 so they could get there quicker.

"Hello. Yeah, my family is dying. I'm riding down 25th St. I need an ambulance. He's slipping away," I said.

"We're sending one out right now," said the dispatcher."

"We're almost there. Just hold on little brother," I said.

"Ta, man__, make sure you look out for my kids and my little brothers and my BM, alright?"

Then he handed me his phone and keys and said that the safe combination is under 'safety.'

"Man, make sure you give my Boo, Saree, some dollars and tell her that I will always love her."

Black started coughing up blood.

"Man, don't do this dude. You gone be alright, little brother. Just hold on," I said.

"Oh yeah, Ta," Black said.

"What's up, bohhy?" I said to Black, then under my breath, "Where the fuck is the ambulance?"

"Ta," Black said again.

"I'm here, Black."

"It was Jackie Robinson," Black said.

"Huh?"

"Yeah. Jackie Robinson was the first Black player in the Major League"

"Right, right. See you here, my nigga. You still here. Just hold on."

"Ta, P.F.L. for life, right?"

"Yeah P.F.L., my nigga."

And right there I felt my nigga's life slip away. And I heard when you die from a gunshot, the bullets makes you feel hot, then cold, then nothing at all.

Mostly all of me died when my nigga got killed. The only part of me that was alive was the part that he saved in that shoot out. I ain't even want to live no more. But I owe this nigga to live because that bullet was meant for me.

When the ambulance pulled up, my nigga was DOA.

Dead.

    On.

        Arrival.

## Chapter 33

When I went to Saree's house I had a quarter of the money in a duffle bag, blood on my shirt, looking completely lost.

You know how sometimes you can feel a bad vibe before you hear about it? Well, this was one of those times. Saree started crying so loud before one word even came out of my mouth.

"I told him that you was bad company. Get out of here, Ta. I don't want no money. I just want my Black back. I hate you. I hate you!" Saree screamed. I just dropped the bag on the porch and blocked the punches.

"Sorry, Ma." Then I walked away. I mean she just met this dude; so how did she think I felt? Plus, it added to the pain to see her like that. Now I was on some ra, ra shit, feeling like anybody can get it. I definitely can't tell his baby's mother, but I gots to drop her off this money.

"Tona," I said, with my head down.

"I already heard, Ta. The hospital called me already."

She was crying low and silently. "He wanted you to have this," I said, handing her a bag of money.

"Thank you very much. But check, it's not your fault. But if you continue being out here, Ta, then the same thing is going to happen to you," Tona said.

"Yeah, he told me to make sure you get this," I said.

"Change the subject if you want, but I'm telling you; slow down out there, Ta."

"Alright. I believe what you say, Tona. But I gots to go. Sorry again. Take care alright?"

# Chapter 34

I was sitting on $140,000, sixty thousand short of my goal, and me and Felicia was already about to leave. But this incident made it official. It was two days after my nigga was gone and the funeral was in three more days. And right after that, we planned on being gone.

Saree had checked into a mental ward. This was her third encounter with death; fourth, including her brother's death.

Come to find out, she been had money and she never set anybody up or nothing. The money that she was getting was from Victims of Crimes for her being too close to violent scenes. This last one had taken her over the top. She really had love for my nigga and couldn't handle him being dead. All she kept saying for three days straight was she was cursed and that her soulmate was gone.

Felicia wasn't good either. She knew how much love that I had for my ace boon coon. And this dude was like a little brother to me. She tried to stay strong for me. Then her friend had finally found happiness in someone that she really loved and he had got taken away from her. "I pray that she'll come around," Felicia said.

'I might as well bang all the tree that I can in the next few days until we leave after the funeral' I thought. I dipped a square and lit it up.

"Man, Ta, pass that square, my nigga."

I looked over to the passenger seat. Damn. It ain't even nobody sitting next to me. I swear for a minute that nigga was next to me riding shotgun still.

"Hello."

"Yeah, Rico. What's up? This Blake. What's up with you?"

"Not too much, B. What's happening?" Rico said.

"Eli's dead."

"Eli's dead? How the fuck that happen?" Rico asked, putting his food tray to the side.

"He jumped the gun and tried to roll on dude but them niggas pent his move, and they started firing shots, too," Blake said.

"So did he hit the nigga, Ta?" Rico asked.

"I don't know. But I do know for sure about his right-hand man, Black__, that nigga's dead."

"R.I.P. my nigga, Eli. And as long as Black's dead, I know that bitch is hurting. But still I gots to handle that nigga, Ta," Rico said

Peaches had been walking by when she heard some familiar names. She stopped and quietly listened to the conversation. She stayed quiet until her shift ended, but as soon as she got off, she made a call.

"Hello, Ta, what's up?"

"What's up?" I said.

"Where you at, Ta?" Peaches asked. "I need to see you."

"Ma, I wasn't planning on doing nothing small tonight," I said, yawning. I was feeling tired. "Shiit, I'm silking right now with my girl, looking at these pictures that we took at the Phase," I added.

"Shhiit, I got something important to tell you, Ta. Man, *you never know* who's listening, right?" Peaches said. "Ta, just come please! Can you meet me at the Gyro house?" she asked.

"That's where you at? Alright," I said. "I'll be there in ten minutes."

I lit up another dippy and took a squig of Hen and poured out some on the curve for my nigga.

I met Peaches inside the Gyro house. She had a two-chair table and had already ordered our food.

"Ta, remember when I told you 'bout my one patient that be stressing me out?"

"Yeah, kinda. What about him?" I asked.

"Well, I overheard him telling somebody about, well, let's just say that he sent somebody to kill you and Black," Peaches said.

"Ma, how much of that weed have you been smoking?" I asked.

"Naw Ta, for real. He said yo' name and he said Black's name and that it was good that Black was dead," she said.

"Huh?" I said, wanting to see where she was going with this.

"But he said, 'Eli's dead,' and that kinda threw me off, 'cause I didn't remember y'all being with nobody named Eli."

"Eli?" I said. "What's this nigga's name?"

"Rico. Rico Davis. In for bullet wounds to the abdomen and legs. He starts physical therapy next week," she told me. "So Ta, you gone call the police, right?" She had a concerned look on her face.

"I don't know. Look, Ma, I need you to do something for me," I said. I was already plotting.

"I'll do whatever you need me to do."

"Alright then. I need a few things from the hospital," I told her.

"Ta, you gone try to handle this yourself? I knew it. I knew. I shouldn't have told you. You trying to get yourself in trouble," cried Peaches.

"If you can't do it, then you just can't do it, Ma. It ain't shit," I said, looking salty and shaking my head.

A tear dropped from my eyes out of pain and I started biting down on my lip.

"Alright, Ta. What exactly do you need? I know that was yo nigga, right?" Peaches said.

A simple nod, kinda ashamed for her to catch that tear, mixed with a smirk. "This is what I need." I semi told her my plan. Just what she needed to know.

"Okay. I got you, Boo. Bet," Peaches said.

"Hello," I said. I made a call to my nigga.

"What up? This Slick, bohhy. How are you feeling?"

"Not too kosher, my nigga. What's happening, doe? That's fucked up what happened to my little nigga, doe, right?" I said.

"Yeah, and you know that was my little nigga, too. R.I.P. his soul. And I need to give his moms or his baby's moms back this deposit," Slick said.

"Man, don't worry 'bout that shit," I said.

"So, man, do you know who did that shit?" Slick asked.

"I mean, I got an idea."

"Well, what's up then, nigga? What you talking 'bout doing?"

"Shiit, you already know."

"I want to ride, too. So come get me, my nigga, and I'ma help you get yo man," Slick said.

"Alright, I'm 'bout to come holla at you right now."

I met Slick at my house and told him what all he needed to do.

"So you got all the shit? Or do you need me to go get it?" Slick said.

I said, "Man, I got everything. I just need you to bring your hammer."

"Alright, that's easy to remember, 'cause I wear that thang like boxer shorts, my Nigga," Slick said, flashing his chrome piece.

"Alright then. But listen up, Slick, 'cause this shit might not be easy." See, I ain't really give a fuck, but I wasn't trying to get nobody else jammed up. "Slick, go do you, and we'll hook up in a couple of hours." We both dapped each other up.

🌿  🌿  🌿  🌿  🌿  🌿  🌿

"Hey, Bay, I got your clothes ready for the funeral, okay? I know this is hard on you. And I packed up some of our stuff," Felicia said. "Ta, if you want to talk about it then I'm listening," she added.

"Naw, Ma, I'm cool, for real. I mean everybody gotta go someday. And after the funeral we're on the first thing smoking. Alright, Bay? And leave all this bullshit behind us, you know?" But I was hurting, doe. I just couldn't talk about it.

"So you're gonna stay in tonight, right?" Felicia asked from the bathroom. She was touching up her hair. "We already have enough money, so we don't need nothing else."

"Yeah, you're right, Bay," I said. "Where you going?"

"I'm going to visit my friend. They won't let her out the mental institution."

"You mean the crazy house?" I asked.

"Ta, don't call it the crazy house. Why do you always gotta say mean stuff? She's been going through a lot and I've never seen her like this before. Period."

"Damn. Come here, Ma. Look. I'm sorry, Bay. And I ain't trying to diss yo friend. I like your friend. So look, why don't you see if you can sign her out, and she can come live with us until she get healthy," I said.

"Ta, is you serious?"

"Hell yeah. That's yo girl, right? Then we'll take care of her like family," I explained.

"I'ma see what I can do as soon as I go down there. Ta, I love you, Boo, you know that? You can be so sweet at times. Let me get going so I can beat the traffic. Oh yeah, we only got two more days before we leave so just make sure that you don't go anywhere," Felicia said.

"Okay, Ma."

"Promise me," Felicia said. She kissed me gently on the lips.

"I promise, Boo," I said.

*'But if you know like I know, a nigga gots to ride tonight.'*

## Chapter 35

"Yeah, Slick. What's up?" I had gone to his house.

"Shiit, what's up?" he answered back. "Let's do this."

I lit up a dip square. "Man, you want to hit this?" I asked.

"Man, I'm cool. You know I don't smoke that shit," Slick said. But he did have a bottle of Hen.

I opened the trunk of the truck and put the wheelchair in the rental. I had on a paper suit under my clothes and a breathing mask to cover my face up, along with a fake badge, a stethoscope, and doctor clothes, too

"This is what it do, right here," Slick said, amping himself up. Then he looked over. "Hey Ta, get up off that depressed shit, bohhy. Shiit, this is for yo man, right here, Nigga. So you ready to roll?"

"Hell yeah, my nigga. Let's do this shit eyebrow down," I said.

"Man, when is you gone give me some of that good stuff, with yo fine ass?" Rico said.

"Boy relax. You ain't even healthy enough to mess with me yet," Peaches said.

"Shiit, I'm ready to get in that ass if I can't do nothing else," Rico said, grabbing for Peaches' skirt.

She eased away and said, "Well look; maybe I will."

"Huh?" Rico was taken off guard from what he thought he heard her say.

"Yeah, maybe I will get you shot. Oops!" She laughed and covered her mouth. "I mean, *give you a shot*." Peaches leaned over and kissed Rico soft and slow on his forehead.

Slick was pushing me down the hall like I was a patient with a broken leg. One foot was straight out in the wheelchair. I had a towel on my nose with my head tilted to the side like I was in some serious pain. Plus, I had a cover over me, too, playing it off like I was trying to stay warm.

"Alright. She told us that the cameras should flip right about now," Slick said, looking at his watch.

Peaches kissed Rico on the lips this time. "Yeah," she said. "I think I'ma give you a shot as soon as I come back." She walked out the door and left Rico waiting with anticipation.

When I saw Peaches walk out, I had Slick push me in.

"Hey Rico! What's up, bohhy? This Ta from high school, remember? Oh, by the way, here go yo shot," I said as I upped the Mac-10 and sprayed crazy.

*Blidididididid! Blidididididid!*

"Whooo!" I yelled.

Something must have come over me, 'cause when Slick told me, "Let's go," I jumped out the chair on one leg with the 40 Cal and unloaded that whole clip too.

"Bitch ass nigga! There go yo shot. Plural mothafucka."

"Man, let's go. You bullshitting."

I jumped back in the wheelchair and rolled with the crowd. People was running and pushing so we blended in. We made it back to the rental and tears started flowing down my eyes.

"Slick, I got him, right?"

I don't know if I was crying from avenging my nigga's death or the fact that I just ended the last chapter of his life.

They said that Peaches acted so scared that they ended up giving her a month off with pay. She never liked that cocksucka to begin with. I made it home before Felicia did.


"Bay, we gotta finish packing," I said.

"Ta, I've been telling you that for two days now," she said, shaking her head at me. I would have been home but across the street from the mental ward, you know Mt. Lukes? I swear that it was police and firetrucks everywhere."

"Swear? Police everywhere?" I said, trying to sound surprised.

"Yeah, Bay. You would have thought somebody got killed over there," Felicia said, sounding dramatic.

"Killed in the hospital? Bay you been watching too much T.V."

"Shut-up, Ta. Something did happen over there."

"Well, don't worry 'bout it, Ma, 'cause after the funeral we don't have to worry about none of this crazy ass shit that's been going on in this city no more," I said.

"Oh, I meant to tell you. They said that I can sign Saree out tomorrow but it wouldn't be good for her to go to the funeral. I can get Monique to sit with her on the funeral day. But tomorrow we got to get the moving truck and everything," Felicia said.

"Alright, you got it. All of that sounds good."

"Ta, you got some kinda glow on yo' face. What have you been doing?" Felicia asked.

I played it off. "I don't know, Ma. It must be you, Boo. Give me a kiss."

# Chapter 36

The next day we got everything together. I went to see my daughter and my B.M and left twenty five thousand dollars under the pillow. I didn't tell her that I was leaving, doe. Shiit, it wasn't like I was leaving the country.

"I'm sorry 'bout your friend, Ta. I'll send my condolences," Erica said. "I'll drop by the funeral tomorrow and show some support," she added.

"Alright, I'll see you there. And bye, Snookie," I said, while I was rubbing my nose against hers, making her laugh, then handing her off to Erica. I left.

I got with Luth and made a few extra dollars. Then Will called me and told me to meet him at the bar.

I grabbed some Newports from the store and while standing in line the newspaper caught my eye.

"Yeah, let me get one of these papers, too," I said, while I was paying the cashier.

The article read: *'A man was found dead in Walmart parking lot. The gun found on the man was the same gun that killed Larino Austin and Kenneth Rogers.'*

*Damn*, I thought to myself. *The nigga's been trying to kill me for a minute . . .*

I continued reading and it stated *'no link or affiliation with a man getting killed in Mt. Lukes Hospital. The suspect in that case is not found yet.'*

"Yeah. Will, you want your regular, right?" I said. I called him because I needed to find out where he was at.

"That's right youngster, nothing more, nothing less," he said.

I came in and sat at the bar. "What's up, Will?"

It was always a pleasure when I saw him, like back with my Pop's old friend. Will ordered two orange-cranberry and Gooses for me and a couple of doubles of Remy for himself. When he gave me the change he slipped in the five thousand dollars for the pound on the play off side. I had already put the weed under his car seat and locked his car door. After two drinks, it was two more, and then came the brews. Now I was drunk and needed to get some shit off my chest. Will knew it, and being the OG that he was, he was the one that had to hear it. I didn't have the heart to tell my Uncle Keith that I was leaving and what had happened yet, but I could tell Will.

Youngsta, I heard what happened to yo man." Will was sipping on a brew while talking to me. "I can see the pain in yo face man. Let it out, Ta. You can tell me anything."

Man, with that, plus the liquor, I was chopping it.

"I mean, why the fuck did we have guns anyway? We had worked our way up into being real businessmen. I mean, what people you know that's worth $250,000 together, walking and riding around with straps? Why was them niggas always tailing us anyway? Didn't them niggas always set goals too? Or was their goal just to bring us down? What a bullshit job, huh? What did it even matter that we set goals or hustled with poise and manners? Because the truth of the matter was it was still an illegal business. And with an illegal business you're always fair game," I said as I took a gulp of my drink.

"So when I found out that Rico had got my nigga killed, I went to the hospital and bust on that nigga. I made sure that I kept shooting until he was dead. Then I emptied out the other clip 'cause I wished that the nigga was still alive so I could kill him again," I said, shaking my head. "Man, it ain't even have to go down like that. But them niggas took somebody that was like a brother from me."

Will gave me some dap and pulled me to him with a hug.

"I would have did the same thing for my peoples, right?" Will said.

"Right," I replied.

Will held up his glass and said "a toast to loyalty. Brother, don't let that shit stress you. You did what you was supposed to do." He downed his shot. "So get some rest, youngsta, and clear your head out. Bet?" Will said.

"Bet," I said.


For the rest of the day I hit some licks here and there. Mainly the people that was the closest to me; you know, my real peoples.

I went and hollered at Lisa and Ronisa for a minute too. It's crazy how sad times and tragedies can bring everybody together.

"Now where exactly is it at, Ta?" Lisa asked. "Yeah, you know I'ma be there, Sugar. Oooh! I feel so bad about last week, too. But I just couldn't have all that violence and stuff around me."

"I understand, Lisa. You don't have to explain yourself," I said, giving her a tight hug.

"Ta, let me get mentally ready for this. You know I don't usually do funerals, but I love you guys, okay?" Ronisa said. Then she kissed me on the cheek.

I cut my day short and went back to Felicia's house. The workers had everything packed up. The main thing she told them to leave out was a few blankets to sleep on, four towels and soap, the small radio with the alarm on it, some hygiene products, and our clothes for the funeral.

When I came in the room she whispered, "Shhhh. Be quiet, Ta. Saree just went to sleep and that's what she needed to get her mental state back. The more she rests then the quicker she'll recover according to the doctor."

She has a small flat screen that she watches all day. That was just what she did now since she had flipped out.

"I hate to see her like that," I said.

"It's alright, Ta. I hate it too," Felicia said

"It ain't shit that we can do to get her back to Saree?"

"Ta, we can't just flip a switch and then she'll be back to normal. The doctor said it's a process. Just to make sure that she takes her meds and make sure that she stays away from all dramatic experiences. Violence can easily trigger off her disorder," Felicia explained to me.

I put my head back and sighed. "Man, I had to open my big mouth."

This is gone be a task and a half right here. I did it for my nigga, doe. Yeah, my nigga, Black. His eyes used to light up whenever he was around that girl, so I'ma help her even if it hurts me.

"Ta," Felicia said, bringing me out of my thoughts. "She'll be alright. Quit worrying about everything. And being that you're one of the pallbearers and we got to get up early, you should be in your right mind. So that mean no getting high today or tomorrow before the funeral."

"I can get high, but I'm not gonna smoke for my little homie's sake. It's a respect thing," I said.

"That's right and I love you for that."

Monique came over about 9pm. "Damn, did ya'll get robbed?" she asked. I guess Felicia ain't tell her that we was moving yet."

"Uh! Uhn! Y'all got something going," Monique said.

"We're about to take a trip after the funeral," Felicia said.

"Girrl, I hate you. You are so lucky," Monique said, in a rich girl playful type of way.

"Where's Saree?"

"She's in the guest room."

"Gosh, poor girl, right?"

"I know, but she'll come around," Felicia said, sounding like a Jewish woman from New Jersey.

"Ta, what's going on with you, lover boy?"

"Ahhh! You got jokes, huh? Well, what's up with you, metal mouth?"

"It's Ms. Precious Metal Mouth to you," Monique said, smiling and showing off the platinum and diamonds in her mouth.

"Ta, can I get some weed?" me and Monique said at the same time. We laughed.

"I knew you was about to say that," I said. "I knew that's why you were warming up to me. Alright, give me ten dollars and I'ma show you some love."

"Ta, I don't have ten dollars," Monique said, in a little sister whining type of voice.

"Man, how is y'all gone be a diva crew and you ain't got ten dollars?"

"Naw, for real, Ta. I had to put it in the tank so I could get over here," Monique said, trying to keep a straight face.

"Now that was a fast comeback. In fact, you should be hustling with me thinking that quick. Naw, here you go, lil ma. But be careful. That's some exclusive shit that my man swapped out with me."

I gave her four blunts. "You lucky that I plan on marrying your cousin."

"I know, so that makes me your little cousin."

"My little cousin? Ahhhh, you know you got game right? Well enjoy, 'cause that's coming out yo pay for watching Saree," I said. I was getting a kick out of messing with her. "Naw, I'm kidding, doe, little Cuz. But I got a big day ahead of me tomorrow, so 'good looking out' for sitting with Saree tomorrow."

"Shiiit, I got to, 'cause that's my girl and anybody that's been through hell like her gots to have a heaven coming from *somewhere*. And I'ma be right there when it comes down to her,"

Monique said, finishing up rolling her cigarillo.

"Damn, lil Ma, you alright."

It was about 10:00pm, and I had planned on going to sleep early so I could get up looking fresh. I had got my haircut earlier that day, and I got the Armani suit with the green tie that symbolizes the dollar and the weed. See, we had already lightweight planned our funerals in one of our bullshit conversations but I personally never thought this day would come. Not at least this quick. It was some other things we planned but I didn't try to go all the way with it for the respect of Ms. Rogers, Black's mother. But Ms. Rogers did approve letting Black get buried in his green tie.

Just thinking, doe, I was supposed to be this dude's best man in a wedding, and now I'ma pall bearer for his funeral. Damn. I can truly say that I wasn't eager to see my dude like that. But it will all be over after this.

Felicia fell asleep in my arms, and not from smoking and being high. I felt the realness of her body. She started grinding her ass up against me and pretty soon I was on rock solid.

I made love to her *for the first time*. I started at a normal pace and slowed all the way down like screw rap; a slow trance as she was laid on her back, looking into my eyes while I was feeling the warmth between her thick legs.

Her eyes were hazel, but they were shining like gold and after a while it got intense. Every stroke was sensitive. I got to shaking until I just had to let go. I fell over to the other side of the bed from exhaustion and she rubbed my chest slowly until I fell asleep.

# Chapter 37

*Knock, knock, knock, knock!*

"Eh y'all need to get up. It stormed last night, and some powerlines got knocked loose," Monique said.

Damn! The funeral starts in an hour and we ain't even dressed. We both ran into the bathroom bumping into each other and in each other's way.

"Ma, get out real quick. I gots to piss."

"Go head, boy. I done seen that thang a hundred times," Felicia said, while she was putting on her make up in the mirror.

"For real, Ma. And my stomach is starting to feel queasy."

"Uhhn uh, Ta. You ain't got time to take no shits. You gone be late and you're a part of the funeral. Ta, you probably just nervous. Here." She gave me a couple of ibuprofen and a few valiums. "This will mellow you out," she said.

We finally got dressed and rolled out. When we pulled up at the funeral I seen that it was a lot of black cars everywhere. Ms. Rogers must have ordered security because it looked like police was everywhere too. I got out and opened the door for Felicia and I was on my way in when a detective looking dude said, "You're a real gentleman and that's what today's society is lacking."

Then the dude added, "Oh, by the way, Tashawn, I'll need you to come with me."

"Huh?" I asked out of shock.

"Yeah, you're Tashawn Adams, right? Well if so, I need you to come with me, sir."

"Ahhh! I can't do that. I'm at a funeral for my best friend, my dude," I said, blowing the stranger off like he was nobody and he was just joking with me.

"I know who he is." The stranger was referring to Black. "We've been watching you both for over a month." This stranger was really starting to look like a real detective to me. Then I knew. He showed me his badge and said he needed to ask me some questions.

"Ta, what's going on?" Felicia asked.

"Nothing, Ma. They just want to ask me some questions." I gave her the phone. "The number to the safe is under P.F. Ma," I whispered to her. "And Ma, we ain't staying here either way, so if they keep me then you know where to go, alright Boo?" I looked at the detective. "Officer, can I at least view my man's body?"

He looked at the other detective and nodded. 'Go ahead.'

Damn. I'm viewing the body in handcuffs looking like a straight criminal in front of my nigga's family. Black's mother, Ms. Rogers, asked, "Is there a problem officer? Tashawn has always been a decent person."

"Don't worry, Ms. Rogers. They just want to ask me a few questions."

I stood over my nigga's body and kissed his cheek. I said, "R.I.P., my nigga." Then I *thought of moving my hand in an imaginary cross* type of way since I couldn't use my hands.

I got escorted to the car and then they put me in it. I was quiet for a second, then I broke the silence by asking, "What am I going down for officers?"

"You're a suspect for a murder," the officer that was driving, explained.

"Alright, here we go with this again. Man, it's cool. I'll be out in five days or less. But damn, doe, couldn't y'all of fucked with a nigga on a better day than my nigga's funeral?" I asked. I shook my head and sat back without saying a single word the rest of the way to the police station.

When I got in my cell, I just laid there. The pills had kicked in and I was in a semi-zone. It was a little puzzling. I was wondering what if they really have been watching me for a month. If they was, ain't no telling how much shit I'll be in.

I called Felicia like, "Ma, I don't know what's going on but don't panic, alright."

"Ta, they said that you killed somebody!" Felicia said, with a trembling voice, sounding nervous as ever.

"Ma, they said that last time and what happened? I got out, right? So be cool. Everything's gone be fine."

"What about you not having a bond? They said that you're a flight risk. And why do I got the feeling that they already knew we were moving?"

"I don't know." I thought maybe they did know, but how?

"Don't worry, Felicia. I'm calling my lawyer and everything's going to be fine."

"Ta, promise me that," Felicia said, like she was on the verge of shedding tears.

"I promise," I assured her.

"Ta, don't do this to me. Promise me that you're coming home," she cried.

"Bay, I said that I *promise*."

But I said it only because it was the only word that could ease her mind at that time.

## Chapter 38

After my fifth day being locked up, I ended up getting indicted. Shiit, I had dumb charges, too: aggravated murder, drug trafficking, trafficking with a gun spec, and leaving the scene of a murder. Plus, a bunch of other shit that they threw in to make my case harder to stomach.

I called my lawyer and he told me that they had been watching me but they only got a few sales. The prosecutor says that he has this John Doe that probably won't make it to court if you asked him. So, therefore, he had said, we going for a speedy trial.

"If they got a fake John Doe, then they're trying to scare a nigga into copping out to a plea bargain. So fuck that," I said. "I'm going all the way."

"Is that what you want?" My lawyer said, sounding very confident. "So that's what we'll do."

My girl had to drive two hours just to come to my trial. She showed me pictures of the new house and I couldn't wait to get there. The trial was going good for me. But if what my lawyer said was true, then I couldn't help but keep wondering why hadn't they tried to offer me a deal yet?

*Never mind that*, I thought. *It's time for me to eat this case.*

My excuse for the weed sales was for promoting of the C.D.s that I was selling. That wasn't weed I was selling, I told them. Those were beats. And since they didn't have anything on video, then they had to bite on that. As far as the guns, I never got caught with one. So I never had one. You feel me?

Everything was perfect. A couple of people even hit the stand for me.

"Ta is not that kind of person. And he wouldn't do such a thing," Lisa said. "I've seen bad men before. I've been abused by them. But this guy you're talking about is genuine and more of the younger men need to be more like him," she added.

Then the prosecutor yelled, "Like what? A murderer!"

"Objection! Objection!" My lawyer yelled out. The courtroom flared up.

"Fuck that! He ain't no mudera," Ronisa yelled out.

The judge told the prosecutor that he was out of line and that he's the only one that will be doing the judging in his courtroom.

My confidence was starting to rise. Then they said they had a wiretap which still meant nothing unless someone who was wearing the wire points out the person whose voice it was. Then I found out that they *did* have someone. And out of all people, why did it have to be my OG nigga, Will?

"Man, hell naaaww!" I yelled, when I saw him take the witness stand. I put my head in my hands. I couldn't believe it.

*'The court would like to call William Taylor to the stand.'*

My heart dropped to my feet, through the floor and never came back. Man, I couldn't believe this shit.

"Mr. Taylor, how long have you known the defendant in this case," the prosecutor asked.

"Uhmm, like ten years," Will answered.

"Okay. I'm going to play a recording, and you tell me if the person that's on it is in this courtroom today."

"Man, I can't believe this shit. Dude pose to be like family," I said under my breath.

*"Yeah, Will, you want your regular right?"*

*"That's right youngster, nothing more, nothing less,"* the recording played.

"Okay." The prosecutor stopped the recording. "Is the person that's on this recording with you in this courtroom today? And if so, could you point him out?"

"Yes he is," Will said. Then he pointed directly at me and said, "It was Tashawn Adams. He's sitting right there."

"And how much did he charge you for the exotic weed?" the prosecutor asked.

"Five thousand dollars a pound," Will answered.

"And how many times have you guys completed this type of transaction?"

"At least twenty times in the last three months, "Will answered.

"Okay. Please listen to this."

The prosecutor flipped the tape machine back on.

*"I went in the hospital and bust on that nigga. I made sure that I kept shooting until he was dead. Then I emptied out the other clip 'cause I wished that nigga was still alive so I could kill him again."*

He flipped it off. "Now, Mr. Taylor," the prosecutor said. "Could you tell me who was on the recording that we just listened to? And if he is in this courtroom today?"

"Yes," said Will. "That was Mr. Adams."

And who was Mr. Adams referring to?"

"He was referring to Rico Davis, sir. The man that was murdered," Will said, his head down.

I looked at Will and said, "Damn, Will, not you," not even knowing those words had slipped out of my mouth.

"What! Don't look at me like that, gangsta," Will yelled out. "Ta, what you thought, that you could just get rich off everybody for nothing? Or you can just turn the city into the Wild Wild West? Boy, you was supposed to call the police. You're a man, Tashawn, and we don't need maniacs like you on the streets. So that's right, he told me that he killed Rico Davis in cold blood!" Then the courtroom went into an uproar.

After I heard that, I had heard it all, 'cause see, Will wasn't really trying to be a good Samaritan. Will was trying to get himself out of some shit.

See, what I found out was that Galena was never sick. Will had been pushing coke for years. But see, Will a do crime but Will didn't do time. So he was gonna have to put somebody down. And that somebody just happened to be yours truly.

"You know what they say, don't hate the player, hate the game," Will yelled, over the noise of the courtroom. Then added, "It's some decent people in the world. Maybe this time a give you some time to learn something."

Man, I was on fire. And that was the last thing I heard before the judge slammed that gavel.

"Twenty-five to life."

I didn't budge, still stunned that the dude that I looked up to and treated like an uncle, had just dog walked me across the courtroom. I heard about shit like that happening. But this dude was right in front of my face, killing me in front of everybody. "Man, you a fucking coward, Will! I got on my knees and prayed for your wife. You're a coward and a snitch! Old hoe ass nigga!" I yelled.

"I can live with that," Will shot back, as he was getting escorted out by law officials.

"Reduced to a peasant," I said. I was full of pain and bitterness.

I looked back and Felicia had fainted. I shook my head, my hands cuffed behind my back. I didn't even realize how much time I had gotten until the cell doors closed.

*"Roooomm Booom!"* I threw all my paper work to the floor. Like "fuck! I got cheated in court. This some bullshit!"

# Chapter 39

"Youngsta!" I heard a voice with a Jamaican accent coming from the next cell. "You don't remember me, do you?" it said.

"I don't remember nobody," I said. I was too salty to hold a conversation.

"I heard what just happened in your case, mon. It happened to the best of us, so don't worry about it. By the way, this is Fabian."

"Fabian? Oh the stripper girl's dude," I said, remembering where I knew him from.

"Yeah, mon, Sapphire's friend." He paused. "I was supposed to get back with you, remember?"

"Yeah," I said. "I do remember."

"Mon, I'ma let you get your mind right 'cause you probably don't want to talk right now. Don't tink too hard. Get some rest and talk to me later."

That was cool with me 'cause all I kept thinking about was my girl crying, and my daughter not having a father at all.

Damn. What the fuck was my lawyer doing? Man, he was supposed to know these things. Surprise witnesses. No deals being offered. And what kinda leeway will I have on the appeal side?

This shit was over with. So right then I got on my knees and prayed. I hate to have to do this in this messed up situation, but I did it anyway.

"*Dear God, could you please save a nig?* Naw hold up. I can't say that. Alright here we go. *Dear God, can you please bless me and make a way for me to get out of here? I only did what I thought was right, so could you please save me Lord? Amen.*"

The first night in was the easiest. All the action in the streets, the ripping and running, the hustling, and having sex, the drinking, the arguing, and the stressing, really takes a toll on a body. So I had no problem sleeping that night. My mental and my body was exhausted.

Then they woke me up for morning chow, and from then on every day was bad.

I was locked in a cell for twenty-two hours out the day. We only came out for rec, phone time, and showers. It was real fucked up, but was gonna be like this, I knew, until they sent me off to my parent institution.

"What time can we use the phone?" I asked a C.O.

"Some time later today," he answered.

See that's the fucked up thing about this shit. You don't have control over yo own life.

This particular day, boiled eggs and some hard ass cornflakes was on the menu for the morning meal.

"Rude boy," I called out to the next cell.

"Yeah, mon, what's up?"

"I forgot your name."

"That might be one of your problems," he said. "Anyone who forgets something that is important as a mon's name, is considered to be selfish in my country."

"Well, yeah, but my bad. Shit, I got a lot of shit on my mind."

"Yeah. You, me, and two thousand other inmates in here."

I didn't have a bunky yet, but for some reason, I felt like I needed to talk to somebody.

"Yeah, doe, when I tried to show some love out there I ended up getting burned. So I ain't trying to be selfish or rude, but I'm solo from now on," I said. I folded my arms on the cell door and talked through the crack in the door.

"I got four years for getting caught with twenty pounds," the Jamaican said.

"Damn, that's it?" I asked, wondering how I got so much more time than him.

"Well, time is time, right?" he asked.

"Hell naw, man. They gave me 25 to life. Now that's time, ain't it?"

"Yea, mon, that's pretty heavy. But you gots to keep yo' head up. You can get back on your appeal, right?"

"I don't know," I said, then mumbled under my breath, "I might have to find another way out."

"Mon, that was kinda fucked up how yo dude played you," he said. "Fucking rasclot, pussyclot maggot. Hem don't deserve to breathe, you hear me!" He seemed almost as upset as I was.

"Yeah, but it ain't no use of crying about it now. I shoulda seen that shit coming."

They finally let us use the phones, and going through all the bullshit, I didn't even realize that I was locked up with some of the niggas from the Bricks. Yeah, the same niggas that be down there with Lil' Man.

I dialed up my girl. "What's up? Did you handle that business?"

"Yeah, Ta," she replied.

"You love me still, Boo?" I asked.

"Of course, I do, Ta. Why would you ask that?" *You have 60 seconds on the phone.* The recording cut in on her talking.

"Ta, I miss and love you." Felicia didn't let the recorded message interrupt her.

"Me too, Big Cuz." I could hear Monique hollering in the background.

"Oh yeah, Mo-Mo said she miss you too. She came down to keep me company for a few weeks."

"Yeah. I heard her," I said and chuckled. *You have ten seconds left.*

"Ta," Felicia spoke quickly, "Call me right back. As soon as you hang up. Alright?"

I tried to call right back but the C.O. was tripping.

"Time's up, Adams," he said. Then he went out the door to talk to a white shirt. As soon as he left, two dudes ran up on me.

"That's him, right?" one said. He was the smaller of the two, lean but mean looking.

"Yeah that's him," the other confirmed. That one was all muscle.

I looked around, I don't know why because I knew I was the "him" they were talking about.

"Ta, what's up?" the first one said. "You owe us a few dollars. Like six thousand of them. Plus interest for that stunt that you pulled on my nigga, Lil' Man."

They were goons from the P.J.s.

"Man," I said, waving them off. "I already talked to Lil' Man." I was trying to talk myself out of the shit I knew was coming.

"Bleed, we ain't trying to talk." The muscular one got right up in my face. "You need to let us know how you going to send them ends."

"Listen," I said. "I don't owe you niggas shit and this ain't the right time neither. So beat it."

"What?" The slimmer guy said in an aggressive tone. He walked up on the other side of me.

"Man, you heard me. I don't owe you shit! Bitch ass niggas."

Soon as those words came out, I swung and hit the slimmer guy with a crispy two piece. Then I turned around and tried to slam the other nigga. I scooped 'em and ran him into the phone. Somebody was on the side yelling, 'Let them niggas work one-on-one.' Then someone said, 'Hey, look out for the CO.'

When me and dude hit the deck, two more niggas came out the cut and started swinging punches. They kicked at me, landing a few in my side. I started to feel that shit, too. I thought the beating was about to be crucial but Fabian came out of nowhere with a long ass hawk. "Back up, Botty Boy!" the big one warned Fabian.

"Get the fuck back before I cut you from hear to hear, mon," Fabian said, with threatening swings of the blade.

"Come on, y'all, fall back," one of them niggas from the Bricks said. "Come on, the guards are coming!"

Man, that shit hurt, but right now I needed to feel some pain anyway to let me know that I was still alive.

I went back to the cell biting down on my lip so the CO wouldn't notice the blood in my mouth. Damn, by this time the day was over. No more phone time, showers or rec.

"Man, y'all niggas gone have to do better than that," I yelled out through the crack in the cell door.

"Nigga, fuck you and that punk-ass, Jafaking," yelled back one of the goons.

"Hey, Fabe, them niggas salty, right?"

"Yeah, mon; the drama. I ain't too for it," he said. "The drama, mon. You hear me?"

I sat down on the bunk and read a scripture out of the Bible. I got on my knees again. I asked the Lord to forgive me for all my sins and to take me out of this situation. And even though I couldn't really see it happening, I still had to keep some kind of faith . . .

# Chapter 40

*"Baroooommm Brroom!"*

"Adams you got some company," a CO said, opening up my cell door.

I swear, a young Mexican dude came in the cell acting crazy off the rip. He was looking at the walls. Then dude started looking down at the floor and out the window, touching the bars, like it was nothing he'd ever seen before.

"Nooo!" he cried out, and shook his head. "These cocksuckers just gave me life. I'm not dying in here, Holmes." He just started talking to me. "I got $300,000 that I can't get unless I get back home," my new bunky said to me, talking like we were friends.

*This dude is crazy,* I thought. *How is he gone get some money when he's stuck in here with me?*

"You see this?" he asked me, knocking on the brick wall in the cell. "Not solid."

Then he pulled out a long Phillips screwdriver. I threw up my guards.

"No. I don't have a problem with you, man," he said, "as long as you don't rat me out. I'm 'bout to break out of here. And if you want to come, then it's fine with me." He started running his fingers over the wall.

"Come with you? What do I need to do?" I asked, hesitantly.

"I don't have any contact with the streets, so I'ma need you to get some magazines."

"Magazines?"

"Yeah. Can you help me?"

"Yeah. I got you already," I said.

"Oh, and if I get you out, I need $10,000 from you for the guy to pick us up. If you can't do it, then don't worry 'bout it. I'll go by myself."

"Man, if you get me out, I'll give you $15,000," I said. I licked my lips, my eyes wide with intrigue by 'my new bunky's plan to escape.

"No need, my friend. I don't do my friends like that," he said, picking at the wall with his fingernail. "All I need is what I need for business purposes. And since I need you, that'll make you my partner."

"Man, if you get me out of here, then you're my partner for life," I said.

"Partners for life, huh? It's kinda cheesy, but I like it."

I started giggling. What kind of luck was this? "By the way," I said, "What do they call you?"

"My friends call me, Blue."

*Damn, how coincidental is that?* I thought. Just like my nigga. His nickname was a color.

"Okay, my Man," I said. "That's what's up." I stuck out my hand to Blue to shake on being all the way in. He shook my hand with a firm grip.

Blue started chiseling while I was knocking on the wall, making beats. Dude two cells down started spitting raps, not knowing that he was helping me out. The next day on the phone I told Felicia that I needed more magazines.

"Ta, I miss you," Felicia whispered into the phone.

"I miss you, too, Boo. You still coming to visit, right?"

"Yeah," she said. "I'm already coming in two days."

Me and Blue put up the posters and he predicted that we'd get shipped out in thirty days, but this should only take two weeks. And somehow he came up with some other tools. When Felicia came to visit I told her the plan.

"Man, I need you to be parked on the side street, right there, Ma." I pointed out the window of the Visitor's Room. "And you got to be there because I only got one try."

I could see that she wasn't up for this type of shit. She started shaking. "Ta, your lawyer said that you might get some time back on your appeal."

"Ma, fuck my lawyer and fuck that appeal." I leaned in and talked low to her. "Ma, these people a let your brains rot in here. They already cheated me in court. Why didn't he try to get me a deal? Or why didn't he let me know how serious the witness was? It was just like he was saying, "Oh, my bad, Tashawn. Your life just got taken away from you, but you might can get it back on an appeal." I shook my head hard. "Ma, you don't get it, do you? I'ma die in this bitch unless you be right there. They're watching my moves, so I can't get visits from anybody else but family in this bitch. This is my only chance. After we leave here, it's maximum security levels, meaning it's over," I said. I was campaigning, making sure she was getting my point.

"Okay, Ta. You said in thirteen days from now?" she asked.

"Yeah. And I'll call you to make sure you're ready."

"Okay. Smooches," she said. But I could hear her voice cracking. I knew she was scared

"Smooches," I said, giving her a soft kiss on the lips.

"I don't like this, Ta."

"Me either," I said. I gave her a tight hug trying to make her feel more secure and relaxed.

A week and a half passed and we went at that wall every day. We could start seeing pipes.

"Alright, right on time." Blue's excitement showed in every part of his body.

One day before we were about to bounce, it was a hole in the wall big enough for us to slide through. I called my girl's phone and heard, "The number that you are trying to reach has been temporarily disconnected or changed"

"What! Damn! I can't believe that shit," I said and slammed the receiver down.

On top of that, at mail call I got a postcard. It read, "I'm sorry, Ta, how things worked out. I had to go with my heart, so go with yours." It was a picture of some other looking country.

"I guess I'll see ya, when I see you." It was signed, Felicia.

"Hey partner, what you get a love letter?" Blue said, joking around.

I put it down and said, "Yeah," trying to play it off, but I'm sure anyone could see the pain and hurt in my face. I couldn't let Blue know that things wasn't going as planned. Now I was ready to do this bitch and she ups and bounce on me after she robbed me for my dough. She supposed to love me. My pain turned to fire. Now, I'ma still go, and I'll get Blue that money somehow 'cause I know that I still got some cash out there somewhere.

Four-thirty one morning, when it was still dark outside, Blue said, "Element of surprise, when everybody's sleepy and really don't feel like being here."

Blue slid out and then I slid out behind him. It ain't take no time to kick the rest of the block out. "Ha! Just like I thought," Blue said. "It's thin!"

We pushed through and jumped out and hit the barbwire fence with the wool blankets and jumped the fence.

"Leave the blankets behind, Ta. We got to get to the street." And that's when we saw Blue's man.

"Nobody gets in here unless you have $10,000." He looked at me and then Blue turned and looked at me.

"Man, I gots to go and get it," I said. I was nervous about it, but I didn't want him to know. "Don't worry about it."

Blue's homie was like, "What the fuck going on, Blue? I was told not to let you in unless you got the money."

"Holmes, I kept my end of the bargain," Blue said. "So what happened to you keeping up your end of the deal?" He looked at me straight in the eye. "What happened to *partners for life?*" He had a disappointed look on his face.

The driver shook his head. "You know what? Come on get in, Blue." And then he pulled out a .357 revolver and pointed it right at my face. I'm 'bout to smoke this disloyal bastard."

I closed my eyes. The barrel of that gun was only two feet away. I didn't run, duck or budge or nothing. At this point I'd rather die than get taken back in.

Soon as dude clicked the hammer on that gun, and I heard it click, I heard a horn blow. I opened my eyes and seen a single bright light speeding toward me. A motorcycle rider pulled up.

"What's up, bohhy?" Then the rider threw me a bag. "You don't have to count it out," the motorcycle rider said. I gave it to Blue.

"See what I told you?" Blue said to the driver. "I knew he was real."

When the person on the bike lifted the shield on the helmet, I saw that it was Sofia.

"Get on, silly. I got to take you to your girl." She was all smiles. "I hope you like Jamaica," she said and smiled again. She looked at me. "C'mon. You looking at me like I'm your guardian Angel or something.

The End

PRESTON K. FRANKLIN
THE AUTHOR

## ABOUT THE AUTHOR

*Preston Kinte Franklin was born, raised and educated in Cleveland, Ohio. 'You Never Know,' is his first book. Yes, you are right! The scenarios, the plot, mastery of street and hip-hop lingo shows you the 'grind' is no stranger to the author. Knowing the game, playing the game and leaving the game, which involved forfeiting his freedom for several years, Franklin used his amazing, natural writing abilities to create this quintessential urban novel.*

*Also a rap artist, Franklin, expanded his literary scope to create this masterpiece of stark imagery and suspense, 'You Never Know'. The book allows readers to truly peep inside the everyday life of hustlers, from interacting with one another, to having to watch their backs, to fashion and grit. Readers care about the author's complex characters as they display their strengths and vulnerabilities. Franklin sends his readers on a journey to witness raw to raw 'real type' hustling, business ventures and the cruelty of the 'game.' Wannabes, or those who are still in the 'game,' will receive a clear message from Franklin that the 'game' itself is colder and stronger than any player could ever hope to be. How deep and far the 'game' can go? 'You Never Know'*

*Franklin resides in Ohio.*

*'You Never Know' by Preston K. Franklin*
*Is available on Amazon.com.*

# *Order Your Copy(ies)…*
# *TODAY!!!*

**PKF Publications**
**Prestonfranklin20@gmail.com**

**Author is available for lectures and book signings at libraries, bookstores, youth events, correction facilities, shelters, etc.**

**prestonfranklin20@gmail.com**

# YOU NEVER KNOW
## by
## Preston K. Franklin

*WHO KNOWS WHAT TOMORROW MAY BRING?*

# WHO KNOWS WHAT AWAITS THE TORMENTED SOUL?

*WHO KNOWS WHAT LIGHT BEAMS FROM THE TORRID TOMORROWS?*

# WHAT FORGIVENESS PEEPS OVER ONE'S HEAD?

WHAT WILL BRING FORTH A GIFT OF INSIGHT?

*WHAT WILL BRING FORTH A NEW SPIRIT?*

*TO THE LIFE OF A MAN*

*EAGER TO BASK IN A NEW BEGINNING...*